THE MAN FROM TH

"A true story of Wor
relates events so dram
the voice of its 14-year-old narrator, Marek, would be gripping given any plot. . . . A survivor of the Warsaw Ghetto, the author neither demonizes nor glorifies, whether portraying Poles and Jews, fighters or collaborators. His refusal to exaggerate gives the story unimpeachable impact." —*Publishers Weekly*

"Riveting in its accounts of smuggling humans and goods through the sewers, of house-to-house fighting through the uprising, and of the personal struggle of one boy for his own beliefs and identity."

—*The Horn Book*, starred review

"A story of individual bravery and national shame that highlights just how hopeless was the fate of the Warsaw Jews as they fought alone and heroically against the Nazi war machine."

—*School Library Journal*, starred review

Winner of the National Jewish Book Award
Winner of the Mildred L. Batchelder Award
ALA Notable Book
An ALA Best Book for Young Adults
NCSS-CBC Notable Children's Trade Book
IBBY Honor Book

OTHER PUFFIN BOOKS ABOUT WORLD WAR II

Andi's War Billi Rosen
Anna Is Still Here Ida Vos
Between Two Worlds Joan Lingard
The Devil in Vienna Doris Orgel
The Devil's Arithmetic Jane Yolen
Friedrich Hans Peter Richter
Grace in the Wilderness Aranka Siegal
Hide and Seek Ida Vos
I Am a Star Inge Auerbacher
I Was There Hans Peter Richter
Lydia, Queen of Palestine Uri Orlev
Mischling, Second Degree Ilse Koehn
A Pocket Full of Seeds Marilyn Sachs
Sheltering Rebecca Mary Baylis-White
To Life Ruth Minsky Sender
Touch Wood Renée Roth-Hano
Transport 7-41-R T. Degens
Tug of War Joan Lingard
Twenty and Ten Claire Huchet Bishop
Upon the Head of the Goat Aranka Siegal

The Man from the Other Side

Uri Orlev

Translated from the Hebrew by Hillel Halkin

PUFFIN BOOKS

PUFFIN BOOKS
Published by the Penguin Group
Penguin Books USA Inc., 375 Hudson Street, New York, New York 10014, U.S.A.
Penguin Books Ltd, 27 Wrights Lane, London W8 5TZ, England
Penguin Books Australia Ltd, Ringwood, Victoria, Australia
Penguin Books Canada Ltd, 10 Alcorn Avenue, Toronto, Ontario, Canada M4V 3B2
Penguin Books (N.Z.) Ltd, 182-190 Wairau Road, Auckland 10, New Zealand

Penguin Books Ltd, Registered Offices: Harmondsworth, Middlesex, England

First published in Israel as *Ish min ha-tsad ha-aher* by the Domino Press, 1989
First published in the United States of America by Houghton Mifflin Company, 1991
Published in Puffin Books, 1995

9 10 8

LIBRARY OF CONGRESS CATALOGING-IN-PUBLICATION DATA
Orlev, Uri.
[Ish min ha-tsad ha-aher. English]
The man from the other side / Uri Orlev; translated from the Hebrew by Hillel Halkin. p. cm.
Translation of: Ish min ha-tsad ha-aher.
Summary: Living on the outskirts of the Warsaw Ghetto during World War II,
fourteen-year-old Marek and his grandparents shelter a Jewish
man in the days before the Jewish uprising.
ISBN 0-14-037088-9
1. World War, 1939-1945—Poland—Juvenile fiction. 2. Holocaust,
Jewish (1939-1945)—Poland—Juvenile fiction.
[1. World War, 1939-1945—Poland—Fiction. 2. Holocaust, Jewish (1939-1945)—Poland—Fiction.
3. Jews—Poland—Fiction. 4. Poland—History—Occupation, 1939-1945—Fiction.] I. Title.
PZ7.O633Man 1995 [Fic]—dc20 94-30189 CIP AC

Printed in the United States of America

Contents

A Word About My Friend Marek

While watching the evening news one day early last spring, I saw some shots of the smoking wreckage of a Polish airliner that had crashed near Warsaw. The passengers and crew were all killed. Only later did I find out that Marek was among them.

Marek was a Polish newspaperman I became friendly with when he visited Israel. We met by chance at the home of mutual friends. We spent the evening drinking vodka, and being about the same age, we were soon reliving memories of the Nazi-occupied Warsaw of our childhood. One reminiscence led to another, and we were hardly aware of time passing as the bottle of vodka grew empty. When we parted in the wee hours of the morning, I said to him, "I have an idea. Why don't I take you on a trip up north? I don't mind taking off a few days from work." He was happy to accept and we shook hands warmly on it.

I awoke the next day with a hangover, swearing at my rashness. I tried to think of an excuse to beg off, of some sudden illness or other calamity, but when I heard his excited voice on the telephone I knew that I couldn't back out. And so, pretending to be looking forward to it while secretly mourning the lost days that could have been put to a thousand better uses, I set out with him from Jerusalem.

By the first evening, however, I was over my regrets, and during the days of sightseeing that followed in the Galilee and Golan Heights, our talk ranged back and forth in space and time without a dull moment. I told Marek about Israel, its history and its problems, and he continued to tell me about his childhood, from which emerged a story that intrigued me more and more. In the end we spent four memorable days together, and upon returning to Jerusalem I jotted down some notes with the thought of making a book out of them. Of course, I would have asked for his permission, but he never gave me the chance. Perhaps he read my thoughts. In any case, he phoned and made me promise not to put his story in writing.

"How did you know that's what I wanted to do?" I asked. And I added, "To tell you the truth, I hate to pass up a good story, but I'm thrilled if this means you've decided to write it yourself."

"Lord, no . . ." He sounded alarmed. "It's just that in Poland . . . I mean, if anyone got wind of it . . ."

"Such as whom?" I asked.

"Anyone. My family. My friends. The government." He paused for a moment. "Even my wife. Nobody knows my background. That's still a very sensitive subject there."

"But if I wrote about it in Hebrew," I ventured, "no one in Poland could read it."

"Sooner or later it would reach us," he said. "I want you to promise me."

I had no choice but to give him my word.

A week later he called to say goodbye. He told me about his last days in Israel and reminded me of my vow.

"I can't say I'm happy about it," I said, "but you can count on me to keep my promise. Although only," I joked, "as long as you're alive."

"Agreed!" he laughed. "Now you have a reason to outlive me."

We parted with the resolution to meet again in Warsaw.

But the last laugh was fate's. Barely two months have passed since then and here I am sitting down to write his story.

Jerusalem, 1987

1

Down in the Sewers

I clearly remember the day my mother was convinced to let me go down into the sewers. After work my stepfather, who was a superintendent in the department of sanitation, made extra money by smuggling food into the Jewish ghetto. The Jews penned up there were literally dying of hunger and were ready to pay almost anything for something to eat.

There were just three of us in the family: my mother, my stepfather, and me.

I heard them discussing it one night until their conversation turned into one of their rare arguments. My stepfather wanted me to help him with the smuggling, since he was already carrying as much food as he could. It was high time, he told my mother, that I did something to help out.

"He's not a boy anymore," I heard him say. "He may be only fourteen, but he's got the strength of a twenty-year-old."

My mother was dead set against it, because she thought it was too dangerous. With my ear pressed to a hollow in the wall through which I could hear them better, I felt a twinge of fear. I had always pictured the sewers as a ghastly underground world beneath the streets and houses of the city, the closest thing to hell I could imagine. And I didn't like my stepfather, either. Just the thought of him made me smell sewage.

Once I was over my first fright, however, it seemed an adventure. Not a single one of my friends in school or on the block had ever dreamed of such an adventure.

I listened tensely to the argument. The more my mother was against it, the more I was for it. My stepfather explained to her that he couldn't ask anyone else: not her brother, because he would want to cut the doorman (with whom he had shady dealings of his own) in on it, and not any of his friends, because there wasn't a single one of them who wouldn't blab for a price. "Only the boy can be trusted," he said.

So I was still a "boy" after all!

Little by little, though, my mother's resistance crumbled. Finally she agreed, provided my stepfather didn't involve me in any "shenanigans."

At breakfast the next morning she said she had something important to tell me. I acted surprised.

"It's time you helped Antony carry food to the ghetto through the sewers."

"Is that all?" I asked.

Even if it wasn't news to me, I felt excited.

"We'll discuss the details tonight with Antony," said my mother, sending me off to school.

Over supper my mother asked my stepfather to explain what I would have to do. Antony shrugged and said there was nothing to explain. "He'll see for himself soon enough," he said while continuing to eat. My stepfather was the silent type.

The next evening he took me down into the sewers.

I put on a pair of his old boots, which my mother carefully greased and padded with old rags to make them fit better, since they were a bit big on me. Then my stepfather put on the miner's helmet that he always wore, my mother checked the stairway to see that the coast was clear, and the two of us descended to the basement, where sacks of food were waiting.

I hadn't known until then how Antony entered the city sewer system. I had always wondered how he could smuggle anything under the noses of his fellow workers. Though it did not seem particularly logical, I had thought that perhaps there were special manholes known only to maintenance men and superintendents like himself. That is, there were ordinary manholes on every street corner — in the winter I had often seen the street cleaners dump piles of snow down them — but there was obviously no way of smuggling food through them, neither before nor after the night curfew, without being caught. Now, however, I discovered that my stepfather had his own private entrance in our basement.

I helped him move some sacks of coal into a corner. When he swept away the coal dust left behind, a trap door emerged that led straight into the sewers.

He climbed down a metal ladder and I followed by the light of the lamp on his helmet. My mother handed me a sack for him and then another for myself. At first I didn't think it was heavy, though I could see from her look that she thought otherwise. But she didn't say anything. She just called down "Good luck!" and shut the trap door above us.

The place was wet, slippery, and smelly, and there were fumes rising in the shaft of light from Antony's lamp. To be honest, my first instinct was to turn around and climb back out. But I didn't. It would have made me look pretty bad. I was ready to put up with a lot worse before I would give my stepfather the satisfaction of laughing at me.

The first part was easy. We walked along the edge of a gutter flowing with sewage, and though the sack on my back kept getting heavier, I thought I would be all right. My biggest worry was that Antony hadn't told me how long it would take. And maybe he didn't know himself, because that night he was going to some new customers, via a different route. After a while, though, we reached a point where we had to stoop and wade through the sewage, which first came up to our ankles and then to our knees. The worst part, in which we practically had to crawl through a conduit between two main sewers, was luckily short, because I couldn't have stood it much longer. I can remember feeling my hands turn to stone, and I was sure that in another minute my fingers would open by themselves and drop the sack. My feet were shaking, perhaps because I wasn't used to walking doubled over for so long, and I was out of breath. I didn't say a word, though. I would rather have died than told my stepfather I needed to rest.

At last we came to a recess in the wall of the tunnel that had some boards in it. Antony took one of them, propped it up diagonally, and laid his sack on it. Then he propped up another board for my sack and the two of us sat down to take a break. After he had smoked a cigarette in silence, we got to our feet again and continued, he first and me dragging after him. It wasn't until our second break that he bothered to speak to me.

"Don't think it isn't hard for me too, Marek," he said.

"How do you do it?" I gasped.

"By trying not to think. I just empty my head and think of nothing but the next few steps, as if they're all that's left. And when I've taken them, I think of a few more steps. Or else I concentrate on lifting my feet one after another. I block out everything else."

Little by little I learned to empty my head too until I understood what he meant. I suppose my body grew stronger and more used to it also. Sometimes I said a prayer over and over to myself, like the old women who ticked off rosaries in church. I was sorry I couldn't brag to my friends about it, but my mother and stepfather had warned me that I had better keep my mouth shut if I cared for our lives.

I hated those trips through the sewers from the start, but I had to take them. My stepfather was right: it was time I helped out. In fact, each time we brought back lots of money, some in American dollars, British pounds, and even gold coins. Now and then I had attacks of claustrophobia, sudden bouts of fear in which I felt that the tunnel was about to collapse and bury me underground. Fortunately, that didn't happen often. And yet oddly enough, I'm still prone to such attacks even now — in elevators, for instance, though I never know in advance when one is coming on.

My stepfather had worked in the sewer system since he was young, but he was made a district superintendent only when the Germans captured Warsaw, because both the superintendent before him and his assistant were killed in the German air raids. Antony knew the maze of the sewer system as well as I knew my way to school and back. He even knew about sewers that were no longer in use or had been sealed off by cave-ins from the air raids, so that they didn't even appear on the department of sanitation's own maps.

Which doesn't mean that my mother was wrong to be worried.

Yet it's true that no one could have known we were down there apart from other smugglers — and we never encountered any. In theory, perhaps, some sanitation worker on an emergency repair job might have run into us too, but that never happened either. Antony was sure that no one suspected him. The only possible informers were the Jews through whose basement we entered and left the ghetto, and they needed the food and made a profit by reselling part of it. Besides, they didn't know our real names or address, although if the Gestapo ever caught us, that wouldn't have been hard to find out. Maybe my stepfather wouldn't have talked, but I'm sure I would have.

In the end, though, we were discovered by a fellow worker of Antony's, a man named Krol. That's when I first understood why Antony had told my mother that first night that he couldn't trust anyone, not even my uncle.

But that's what wartime is like: suddenly you find out that everything you've thought about your friends, or your neighbors, or your relatives, is wrong. Anyone at all can inform on you or get you into hot water, because when someone is frightened, or hungry, or desperate for money, he's no longer the same person.

My mother liked to say that Antony talked tough but would never hurt a fly. That's not what happened with Krol, though. He must have suspected Antony for quite some time. Perhaps it started with his noticing how much food Antony was buying. We were lucky that he kept it to himself and took the secret with him when he died — and to a Jewish burial at that!

It happened late one night. We were struggling along with our sacks of food when suddenly we heard an ugly laugh and someone shined a flashlight on us.

It was Pan Krol. He had waited for us to approach before switching on his light, and now he stood in a bend of the sewer and said with a snicker that from now on we could split our profits with him. Antony didn't bat an eye. As if meeting Pan Krol in a sewer were the most natural thing in the world, he said perfectly matter-of-factly, "Fair enough. But that means we split the investment and the risk, too."

It certainly seemed fair to me. But Pan Krol didn't think so. He wanted to blackmail us, for us to pay him just to keep his mouth shut.

"Go wait for me beyond that bend, Marek," Antony said to me. "I need to talk to Pan Krol in private."

He lit the way to the bend for me. As soon as I was around it — naturally, I peeked to see what was happening — he put down his sack in the sewage, since there was nowhere else for it, and stepped up to Pan Krol. I was sure he only wanted to have a quiet word with him, but suddenly Krol was face down in the sewer and only then did I see the knife in Antony's hand. He wiped it off on Krol's clothes, tucked it back into his jacket, took out a white armband with a blue Star of David like the ones worn by the Jews, and tied it around Krol's arm. We always took a few such armbands with us because we had to wear them ourselves on our way through the ghetto.

Antony started to kick Krol into the gutter, thought better of it, bent down, went through the dead man's pockets, and took what I supposed was some money from them. Then he tore up some pieces of paper, threw them into the sewage, glanced in my direction, and gave Krol a swift kick that sent him floating off on the current. Only then did he call me. I pretended not to hear him the first time and made him call again before I came and helped him shoulder his sack. I never breathed a word of what I saw to anyone, not even to my mother.

In the ghetto we would surface through a basement

on Leszno Street and walk from there with our sacks down Karmelicka Street. I'll never forget those few blocks, though they weren't very long. The Jews at Leszno Street would give us fresh clothes to keep us from smelling (I needn't tell you how it felt to put our stinking wet pants and shirts back on before heading home through the sewers), and we stepped out into the street looking like any Jew. Sometimes I would pretend I was a Jew, just to see what it felt like. Still, whenever we passed a vantage point from which I could glimpse the Polish side of the ghetto wall, I made sure to look.

Each time I came back from a trip to the ghetto I had bad dreams at night, most often about the children who pleaded for food, or else about the beggars who lay drooling on the sidewalks. My stepfather said they filled their mouths with soapsuds to make people feel sorry for them, but sometimes they were covered with newspapers because they were dead. Antony told me not to look at the children, since he saw how badly I wanted to give them something to eat. If anyone discovered that we were smuggling food, he said, we would be finished. True, there were big-time smugglers who worked in organized gangs and weren't afraid of anything, because they had connections with the Polish police and even with the Germans, who let them come and go through their checkpoints. But we were "free-lancers" who had to hope that the sewers would keep our secret.

Sometimes the main streets of the ghetto were so

crowded that we could hardly move. Jewish policemen directed the traffic, keeping one direction to the right and the other to the left, because otherwise there would have been a hopeless jam.

I can remember my disbelief the first time I saw a Jewish policeman hit a Jewish boy. It must have been on our second trip, because the first one was at night and we didn't venture out. Until then I had thought that only Polish policemen were mean. I never thought Jews could be like that, because my mother had told me that, although they would do anything to strangers (which meant us Poles too), they would never harm one of their own. She said that the Jews always helped one another — but now I saw that their policemen were no better than ours. And later on I learned that they had informers and traitors too, just the way we did.

Another thing I couldn't believe on that first walk down Karmelicka Street was all the stores full of delicacies. If I hadn't seen starving children everywhere, I might have thought that the ghetto was a wonderful place to live. Antony explained to me that the corner of Karmelicka and Nowolipie streets where the Hotel Britannia once had stood was a center for the shady dealings of all the rich Jews, money changers, Gestapo agents, smugglers, and various underworld types who hung out there. So did we, because that's where our customers were.

But I haven't finished telling you about my first trip through the sewers.

By the time we arrived, I didn't think I could take another step without collapsing. My stepfather put down his sack, climbed up a ladder, grabbed an iron rod that hung from a rusty chain, and rhythmically tapped it seven times against a metal trap door. He paused and tapped again, and this time the trap door opened.

It worked like this: we telephoned in advance and announced the day and hour we were coming in a coded message that only our customers understood. The telephone we used belonged to someone called "the doctor," a Polish official who worked in a nearby brush factory and was bribed by our customers to relay our message to them. They were three brothers, religious Jews like the ones I had seen in Jewish neighborhoods before the war began. Such people had always seemed strange and ugly to me. Maybe it was their odd clothes, or their beards and sidelocks, or the strange language they spoke, and maybe it was all of those things put together, plus the poverty and congestion they lived in even before the war broke out.

In any case, the first time we arrived in the brothers' basement and I saw them reach down to take our sacks and help us through the trap door, they scared me half to death. We sat down to rest for a minute, and then — after Antony had rubbed his fingers to restore their circulation — we opened our sacks. I took out each item and handed it to Antony to display to the three Jews, who sat muttering in their language with bright eyes. Antony arranged all the bread and cheese and butter and herring and apples and sugar and homemade vodka as neatly as if he were opening a grocery store while I emptied out the sacks, still out of breath from our trip.

Although my stepfather was barely able to read a newspaper, he knew Yiddish. I remember how amazed I was to find that out, because anti-Semitic Poles like him liked to make fun of the way Yiddish sounded — and yet here he was speaking it like a native, with the same funny singsong!

In the course of time Antony mellowed toward the three brothers, but back then he was still very brusque with them. They too grew friendlier once they got to know and trust him, and sometimes served us special Jewish delicacies that were brought down to the basement because we smelled too bad to come upstairs. On our first trip, they were afraid of him and shocked by the price he started out by asking, which was twice what he expected to get (he had warned me in advance not to say a word while he bargained). But they brought us tea and candy when the haggling was over. At first I was afraid to put the candy in my mouth. I thought I might catch something from it, because the Germans had put up signs on the ghetto walls reading in German and in Polish, "Warning! The Area Beyond This Wall Is Infected with Typhus!" I had seen those signs so often that I almost believed them, but the candy was really good, the kind we used to get before the war.

As we came to know the Jews better, Antony sometimes joked as he bargained with them. He was no longer in such a hurry either, so that every item was auctioned off separately. The Jews too grew less scary with time. Perhaps their strangeness had given me the wrong impression, although I certainly didn't think so at first. And even when we were used to bantering with them, I was startled one day when one of them told us a sick joke about the ghetto. Not that it wasn't funny, but I remember thinking that someone whose friends and families had been killed and who might face the same fate any day shouldn't be talking like that.

After the basement on Leszno Street there was a time when we surfaced via the basement of a store on Grzybowska Street. Pan Korek's tavern was to stand opposite this spot later, once the Germans had shipped most of the Jews off in trains to Treblinka and let the Poles have all the empty apartments in what was called "the Little Ghetto." And after Grzybowska Street we entered through the brush factory, whose employees had not been deported because they were making brushes for the German army. Getting there through the sewers took twice as long — two hours with full sacks and an hour returning with empty ones.

Gradually, my feelings toward my stepfather began to change. Part of it had to do with Pan Krol and part with all kinds of other things, like his telling me that carrying the sack was hard for him too. I never saw him slip or fall with it, though, which happened to me a lot in the beginning. Each time we came home my mother sent me straight to the bathtub and then shaved my head, because that was the only way to get the smell of sewage out of it. I didn't want to reek in school or have children asking me questions. "I bet you have lice," they all said when they saw me. "No, I don't," I told them. "I just like the way it looks." Skinheads were the fashion in the upper grades at the time, so perhaps they believed me.

As for the incident with Krol, it may have made me more afraid of Antony, but it also made me feel safer with him, because it gave me the confidence that he could cope with any danger.

When we took the long route to the brush factory, we also took more breaks along the way. Each stop had boards hidden in the wall, and at each my stepfather ceremonially propped one of them up, laid his sack carefully on it, helped me to lay mine down too, and propped up another board for us to sit on. Sometimes he lit a cigarette while I had to pretend I didn't smoke even when he let me have a puff. He didn't know that I was already smoking on the sly, both by myself and with my friends when we went downtown. I looked older than my age and was afraid only of being caught when I was close to home or to school.

There were fourteen stops along the way to the brush factory, although Antony smoked at only three or four of them. After a while he began calling them the "Stations of the Cross," or for short, the "shit stations."

If our sacks were empty, we generally stopped to rest only once on our way back. But they weren't always empty, because that autumn, when most of the ghetto was already evacuated but no Poles had moved into it yet, we often took a detour through a low tunnel that nearly forced us to walk on our knees, exiting at Grzybowska Street. There, before heading home, we ransacked the deserted houses for special items that had been ordered from us earlier or simply for things that we ourselves wanted, such as silverware, dishes, clothing, and linen.

The one time my stepfather didn't take me along with him was when he went to the ghetto to sell arms. He didn't realize that I knew and that I felt left out.

I heard him talking about it to my mother one night. He told her that he had three "pieces" that he wasn't going to sell to the Polish underground because it didn't pay a fair price.

"So who will you sell them to," asked my mother, "gangsters?"

There was a moment of silence and then Antony said, "No. I'll sell them to the Jews."

I could tell by his voice how hurt he was. My mother must have heard it too, because she said she knew he wouldn't really sell guns to gangsters. And he didn't have to, he explained to her, because the Jews would give him seventeen thousand zloty for a single pistol. Why, they would pay him one hundred for every bullet! After that there were some whispers that I couldn't make out, and then a whole lot of smooching that made me cover my head with my pillow.

There was one other kind of merchandise that my stepfather sometimes smuggled, not into the ghetto but out, although strangely enough, he never kept a cent of the money he was paid for it. That was Jewish babies.

By the autumn of 1942, when what was happening to the Jews in Treblinka was no longer a secret, some Jewish families were desperate to save their small children. They would contact us through the three brothers, and Antony would carry their children out of the ghetto in a sack. I myself saw him do it three times, although it may have happened more often, because when I asked him how many babies he had smuggled he said he couldn't remember.

He took only girls, because boys were circumcised and could be identified as Jews. I had to ask him what being circumcised meant, and I didn't believe him when he told me. I was sure it was just another one of his Jewish jokes. I realized he was telling the truth only when I overcame my embarrassment enough to ask my mother, who gave me the same answer.

The first time I saw Antony being handed a baby, I was in shock. He hadn't warned me in advance, and I almost broke into tears like its mother. He never let me know about such things beforehand, because he believed in learning by experience. The baby's mother couldn't stop crying. She undressed it for the doctor, who came to give it a shot in its little behind to make it sleep, and then wrapped it up again, kissed it, and gave it to Antony together with a bag. In the bag, I was told by someone there, were the name and address of the baby's parents and of an aunt in America, so that the child could be returned to its family after the war. "And there's also some money, all of which your father claims is for the mother superior of the convent."

Although Antony looked annoyed when he heard that, he didn't say a word.

He put the baby in his sack and we descended into the sewers. After walking a while I asked him about it, and he told me that he brought the babies to a convent where they were raised to be nuns and good Catholics.

Who kept the documents? I asked.

"Oh, those," he said, as though he had forgotten all about them. He took the papers out of their bag, tore them into little pieces, and threw them into the sewage.

"But suppose its mother lives through the war and looks for it afterwards," I said. "How will she find it?"

Antony didn't think much of the mother's chances of surviving. In the first place, he said, she wasn't young and strong enough, and besides, the Germans would kill all the Jews anyway. He must have felt I wasn't convinced, because he added that it was better for the baby to grow up a Catholic and never know it had Jewish parents. Being Jewish was nothing but trouble. It always had been and always would be — that was something I could see for myself. He was simply doing the baby a favor.

Being a nun was nothing but trouble too, I said. But Antony answered that the convent was really just an orphanage and that no one had to become a nun if she didn't want to "And don't think I'm doing it for the money," he told me. "I really do give every cent to the mother superior."

But if he disliked Jews so much, I asked, why save their babies free of charge?

"You don't understand, Marek," said Antony. "I may not like Jews, but I have nothing against human beings."

2

The Money and the Secret

Sometimes I wonder what would have happened if my mother hadn't caught me the first time. Would I have gone on doing it with Wacek and Janek? I think that if I had gone to confession and told the priest about it, I would have stopped.

In his Sunday sermons our priest sometimes mentioned "our brothers in distress." I knew he meant the Jews. He wasn't like Wacek and Janek's priest, who talked about "kikes" and "Christ killers."

I'm sure that if my mother hadn't told me about my real father, I would sooner or later have gone to confession and told the priest what I did. I actually liked seeing him, and not just because I could say yes when my mother asked me at least once a week: "Marek, have you been to confession?"

It had nothing to do with Antony either, who went to confession like clockwork on the first Thursday of each month. Confession was a way of getting away from all my problems in school and at home and of feeling better about myself. I liked our priest and looked up to him. I never told him about the money, though, because meanwhile I found out about my real father and didn't go to confession anymore. There was no point in going when I couldn't tell the truth and talk about what was most on my mind.

I've already said that Antony didn't have much use for words. He talked a lot only when he was drunk. Once, when I was dragging him home from the tavern, he said to me that no man could keep everything inside him because it would make him sick if he did. That's why he himself told my mother everything, he said, and if he couldn't tell her something, he told it to the priest. It seemed a good time to ask about what kinds of things he couldn't tell her. I thought he might mention Pan Krol, but he surprised me by saying, "I swear to you, Marek, I never go to whores. I love only your mother. And you. Why don't you call me Papa, all right?"

He began to cry like a drunk, because I wouldn't agree to let him legally adopt me. That must have been in early December, before the first snow, three or four months after I started working in the sewers.

The ground was covered with the first white frost of the year and the puddles in the street had frozen. It was early on a Monday morning. I know it must have been a Monday because I had just returned Pan Korek's three-wheel bicycle to the yard behind the tavern.

The streets were almost empty. The children hadn't left for school yet. I chose the longest puddles, gave myself a good head start, and went sliding over them.

I wondered if my mother was right that sliding wore down the soles of your shoes. Suddenly someone called my name and I saw Wacek and Janek. I remember thinking: what the heck are they doing here at this hour? Our school was in the opposite direction. "Those two young punks," my mother used to call them. She had told me to keep away from them, but I didn't. Only, what were they doing out in the street so early? They could have asked me the same question, but I had a good answer. So did they, it turned out, although it took a few minutes to find out what it was.

They weren't exactly friends of mine. They were two grades above me, but since I was big for my age and at least as strong as they were, they occasionally invited me along on their adventures. Sometimes we crossed the Kerbedzia Bridge to the Praga, which was close enough to my grandmother's for me to tell my mother I was going there, and we picked fights with the kids hanging out there. Sometimes we went shoplifting.

I don't think the two of them ever went to confession, which may be why they stole things I didn't dare to. I stole only small things like candy, for which the priest made me say two Ave Marias while adding in a mournful voice, "Thieves come to no good end, my son."

Sometimes, when we were feeling good, Wacek, Janek, and I would teach the little kids in the street "the facts of life," stopping them on their way home from school and telling them where babies came from. Wacek and Janek were good at that kind of thing. My mother said they had no conscience.

Anyway, there I was flying across a frozen puddle on the sidewalk when Wacek and Janek appeared out of nowhere. When I asked them what they were doing out so early, they answered with a nasty grin, "How about you?"

Because they knew. They knew that every Monday I had to return Pan Korek's three-wheeler after pedaling my stepfather home on Sunday night since he regularly got so drunk that he didn't know which foot was which.

They told me that the street we were on was a common escape route for Jews from the ghetto. If they saw someone walking on it early in the morning, trying to act innocent but looking pale and Jewish with eyes that popped out of his sockets, they stepped up to him and said, "Hey, mister, come over here for a minute." If he began to shake all over, they knew for sure he was a Jew.

At first they talked to him nicely to keep from arousing the suspicions of any passers-by who might want a share of the loot. Then they took him into a doorway, shook him down, and cleared out.

Although they made it sound perfectly natural, I was afraid. They assured me that they never turned any Jews in to the Polish police or the Germans, even though they could get a reward for it. They simply "shaved" their victims, that is, took all their money and their valuables. Sometimes they left them enough money to buy food or a streetcar ticket. That meant they still made off with lots of cash, enough to do all kinds of things. They began to laugh so long and so hard that someone opened a window and emptied a bucket of water on the sidewalk near us. Wacek reached for a rock, but just then the doorman appeared and shook his fist at us. We moved down the street while Wacek juggled the rock in his hand, looking for something to throw it at. The target he found was a dog that had the bad luck to pass by. With hardly a whimper it stuck its tail between its legs and ran off. They asked me if I wanted to join them.

"I'm sure it's a sin," I said.

"You can always go to that commie priest of yours and confess," Wacek said.

"Don't be a sucker," said Janek. "They've got lots of diamonds and gold besides the money. Just think what you can buy with it. What are you, a Jew lover or something?"

I certainly didn't want them to think me a sucker or a Jew lover. "But suppose my mother finds out?"

"If you don't tell her, how can she?"

"He's still just a baby," said Wacek. "Let's leave Mama's little boy alone and get going."

I was fourteen and looked like sixteen, and I didn't like being talked about like that. Many of the customers in Pan Korek's tavern talked about robbing Jews who had escaped from the ghetto. I even knew a few toughs who made a regular living from it. And if I didn't tell my mother and Antony, how, really, could they know? I began to think of all the things I could buy. What are you afraid of? I asked myself. It's just this one time. Wacek and Janek will "shave" some Jew anyway, so what difference does it make if I join them?

"All right," I said. Janek slapped me on the back and we went to look for a Jew.

Pretty soon one came along. Although he wasn't walking especially quickly, he looked as though he was in a hurry. He was carrying a briefcase and was pale indeed, although that didn't prove he was a Jew of course. But though he tried to look straight ahead, his eyes kept darting every which way. We steered him into a doorway and said straight-away, "Hand over your money, kike!"

He began to plead with us. If we took all his money, he might as well turn himself in to the Germans. How could he pay for a hide-out or for food? I felt kind of sorry for him and said we should leave him something.

"You can let him have it from your share," said Janek.

And Wacek said to the Jew, "You should be thankful we didn't tear your pockets out to look for diamonds. I'll bet you've got gold coins sewn in your underpants too."

The Jew had a big wad of money on him. Wacek and Janek gave in to me and left him a little. They didn't even take it out of my share. Then they let him go. All I could think about on my way to school was how I could now buy anything I wanted without having to ask my stepfather. Then I began wondering what the two of them did with the money that made them laugh so hard. I was sure from the way they laughed that it must be something dirty. I sat through school planning what I would buy. Each time my hand touched my pocket, I smiled to myself. Yet even then I couldn't stop thinking of the Jew's pale face and eyes. It became harder and harder to get them out of my mind.

I flunked the dictation. And I didn't dare buy a thing on my way home from school. I suddenly felt as if my pocket were on fire with the money. I was afraid to put my hand in it. By tomorrow, I tried telling myself, it won't bother me. But I knew I had done something wrong.

That night my mother read me a bedtime story. Not that I didn't know how to read. I just liked being read aloud to by my mother. If I'm not mistaken, at the time she was reading Victor Hugo's *Les Misérables* in installments.

I was thinking so much about the book when I fell asleep that I forgot to take the money out of my pants.

When I awoke the next morning, the day before already seemed a hazy memory. All that remained of it was the money. I jumped out of bed knowing it would be a great day. Just then I saw my mother pick up my pants and brush them as she did every morning to make sure I went to school looking clean. I could feel myself turn white as a sheet.

"What is all this money, Marek?"

I tried making believe it was nothing. I was good at pretending with people, although until then it was a talent I had never tried out on my mother. It was something I had saved strictly for school or for my stepfather.

The fact was that I hated lying to my mother until the day she died. When she was eighty-three years old and dying I told her a lie about her health, and even though that was something else of course, it was as hard for me as when I was a boy. In the end she always saw through me. If something sounded fishy to her, she would take my face in her hands and look straight into my eyes, deep into them. She was never angry, just sad. But she always knew.

I bent down as though lacing my shoes and said as casually as I could that I had found the money in the street and had forgotten to tell her about it yesterday. I didn't know whom it belonged to. Maybe some smuggler had lost it, because a big wad like that . .

My mother listened in silence. I thought I had talked my way out of it. At-most I would have to make my peace with not buying all the things I wanted, because I would have to give most of the money to my parents. That was just the lull before the storm, though, because my mother suddenly said, "I found a note among the bills." She showed it to me. It read: "Keep the bearer of this note in the apartment until the morning. I'll come to pick him up and pay you. Krupnik."

To this day, whenever the worst is about to happen, I pretend to myself that everything is normal and do my best to find something in the situation, something interesting or funny or odd, that I can peacefully contemplate. During the Russian invasion of

Czechoslovakia in 1968, for example, there was a moment when a Russian soldier angrily aimed his gun at me. And I remember thinking: just look at how that idiot was in such a rush to get dressed when his unit was mustered that he missed a button on his shirt — I'll bet he gets a reprimand. In the end he didn't shoot. I was there as a journalist.

And so, while my mother stood there looking at me, all I could think of was the name Krupnik that had been on the note I hadn't seen. I thought it was the funniest name I had ever heard. I almost looked up from the shoe I was lacing to tell my mother that. "Well," I said, "maybe it wasn't a smuggler. It could have been someone on the run. Maybe someone from the underground."

"Maybe a Jew," said my mother.

"Maybe," I said without blinking.

"You know," said my mother, "I met Wacek's mother in the grocery store the other day. I always told you to keep away from him. And from that friend of his too — they're a pair of young punks. The minute I saw that money, even before I found the note, I thought of something she told me."

I put my school bag down on the floor and sat down. There was still some tea left in my glass. I went over to the table and drank it. It was already cold, which was perhaps why it tasted too sweet. I wanted to ask my mother if tea tasted sweeter when it was cold.

"Wacek's mother told me that for the last several

months he's been going around with too much money," she said. "He's been buying all kinds of things with it and giving her large amounts too. He says it's from working in the marketplace. She never pressed him about it, she told me, because ever since the Germans took her husband she's had trouble making ends meet. As long as it helped pay the food bill. And then one day she ran into Janek's mother. When she told her about how much money Wacek was earning in the marketplace, Janek's mother laughed at her and said that it came from shaking down Jews."

"That doesn't mean — " I began to say. My mother didn't let me finish.

Although I was taller than Mother, I was seated, and now I looked up to see her standing over me. In a voice I had never heard her use before, she said, "You robbed a Jew with them, Marek. Tell me the truth!" I realized that Janek was sure to rat on me anyway. He was the biggest squealer there was, in school too. And so I told the truth.

When I had finished, my mother looked pale. I didn't try to defend myself. What could I have said? That the two of them would have done it anyway? I simply told her everything and said the Jew should have been thankful that we didn't turn him in or tear out his pockets and underpants looking for diamonds or gold.

"Who taught you such nonsense?"

"It's not nonsense. That's where the Jews hide their

valuables when they escape from the ghetto. Wacek and Janek told me."

"How many Jews have you robbed?"

"Just one," I said.

I thought she was going to yell at me. I wasn't used to that, but I was ready for it. In fact, though I didn't think it likely that she would tell my stepfather to beat me, I was ready for anything. Except for what happened. My mother sat down on the floor and started to cry. At the time, all I remember thinking is: what is she sitting on the floor for? Today, though, telling the story to you for the first time in my life, I feel like crying myself.

She cried with great big sobs, the way you cry when something terrible has happened or when you've had a great loss, the way you cry for the death of a child.

I tried lifting her into a chair. Anything to keep her from sitting and crying on the floor! She wasn't hard to pick up, but she pushed me away with all her strength. That frightened me even more. In the end, I managed to get her onto the sofa, where she went right on crying.

And all that time I kept saying "Mama, Mama" without even knowing that I was saying it. She must have been already on the sofa and wiping her nose between gasps when I realized I had been calling her name.

All of a sudden she said, "Why, Jesus was a Jew and so was the Virgin Mary! And Joseph was a Jew too. And John the Baptist. They were all Jews. It says so in the Bible." I was flabbergasted. I had never thought of it that way. And she went on, "What do you think that Jew is going to do without his money? How is he going to save himself? You sentenced him to death. Your father gave his life for human brotherhood, and you, Marek, how could you look him in the eyes now? What will you say to him when you stand before him on Judgment Day?"

She fell silent. I wanted to say something but didn't know what. I had a bitter taste in my mouth like the taste you have when you want to apologize, to explain. But it would only have been a lot of lies and half truths, a pap I would have vomited up and that couldn't have looked very pretty. I felt so guilty that I wanted to hide where nobody could see me, the way I do in a dream I sometimes have in which I'm walking naked in the street. Just then my mother got up, took the wad of money from the table, and threw it at my feet.

"Take your money, you Judas Iscariot!"

I crossed myself automatically. I really was like Judas, who had betrayed Jesus to the Romans for thirty pieces of silver.

I remember wanting to argue that Jesus was not a Jew because he had been baptized, but then I realized that wouldn't have made any difference to the Germans. One Jewish grandparent was enough for them.

My mother handed me my school bag and pushed me toward the door. "Go," she said. "Get out of here. I can't bear the sight of you."

I began to cry. It must have been ages since my mother had last seen me cry. She came over to me and hugged me. I hugged her back hard and said I was sorry and that I would go look for another Jew who had escaped from the ghetto and give the money to him. That scared her enough to say that I should leave it to her to see that the money reached the right hands. She stepped back and gave me a long look as if seeing me for the first time. Then she murmured to herself, "Perhaps I should have told him when he was thirteen, as I promised his father I would."

She looked at me again as if taking my measure and continued, "Maybe the time has come . . . " That's when she told me.

I started out for school, but my feet took me straight to church. I had to pray. I felt as if the sky had fallen. It wasn't possible. And yet my mother would never have invented such a thing just because of the money. I had always believed everything she told me. She never lied to me. She had an honesty you couldn't help but respect, and I don't think a single one of her friends ever suspected her of not being truthful. Still, she *had* lied, or at least not told me the whole truth about my father.

I prayed, mechanically, compulsively, without being able to stop. And as I did I kept examining myself — not from the outside but from within, to see if I was still the same Marek I had been before finding out the truth. Could it be that I had already begun to change and would soon turn into someone else?

Then I stopped praying and continued to kneel, looking at Christ crucified over the altar and wondering whether Wacek, Janek, and I would have taken him for a Jew. I began to talk to my father. It was different from all my other talks with him, which weren't always in church. Sometimes they even took place when walking down the street.

I felt so cold that my teeth chattered. I tried to guess if it was time yet for the school gate to open. Finally, I rose from the floor and sat down on a pew. All this time I had thought I was alone, but now I saw that someone else had entered the church, without my noticing. Or perhaps he had been there praying, because out of the corner of my eye I saw him crossing himself. There was something odd about it that I couldn't put my finger on. Only later, when I was already out in the street, did I realize what it was. It was the way he had crossed himself. He had done it backward!

3

My Father

My mother told me that my father's parents were just like the Jews I knew from Nalewki Street. His own father went around dressed in black and had a beard and sidelocks. My mother saw him only once, when they met by chance in the street, and she never saw my father's mother while my father was alive. That, she explained to me, was because when he married a Christian they sat in mourning for him and pretended afterward that he was dead.

For weeks I tried to form a new picture of my father. It wasn't entirely new. Everything my mother had told me about him over the years was still usable. Things like his height, or the color of his eyes and hair, hadn't changed. All at once, though, I had to see all these things against a new background, you might even say a new stage set, with a different spotlight shining down on them.

Not that I thought of my father all the time. I went on thinking about all the other things that boys thought about too: football, and girls, and school, and fights in the Praga. And working the sewers with

Antony. Every now and then, though, in church or in bed at night, my thoughts returned to him and I instinctively began to talk to the face I had drawn in my imagination.

My starting point was still my mother's descriptions, which I knew by heart. But I couldn't think of my father as Broneslaw Jaworski anymore. Not when his real name was Hayyim Rozenzveig. My father was given his Polish name, as well as his Christian identity and a forged birth certificate, by the Communist party before I was born, before he even knew my mother. He was already on the wanted list then. And without changing his physiognomy, I was beginning to give him a different face. It still looked a lot like the one I had imagined before, but it was different. It wasn't exactly a Jew's face. Picturing it, I knew I still wouldn't suspect him of being Jewish any more than his friends in the party did — a party that I hated in those days and was never able to connect with the brave figure of my father. Still, his expression was no longer the same. Today, I can say that it had even changed for the better. Now there was something tender about it. The cold eyes and stern face of the dedicated Communist who had died under torture without breaking seemed to have become warmer and more human.

Until then I had thought of him the way you think of a comic-book hero, the kind who talks with bubbles around his words, strong and invincible. Whereas the secret my mother told me now made him . . . well, I wouldn't have put it that way as a boy, but today I would say that he became less abstract and more down-to-earth for me, someone who really was born and lived, although in a past that was very distant, since anything more distant than his father's childhood is hardly imaginable to an adolescent.

The more I reimagined him, the more I had to rewrite the whole story of his life, to change my whole conception of him, starting with his childhood. Even then I had the honesty to make myself see him as one of those Jewish boys from Nalewki Street with long sidelocks and skullcaps or hats on their heads who always looked so pale that I felt sorry for them. Sometimes, before the war, I went bargain hunting there with my mother. And yet I consoled myself by thinking: this boy will grow up and become the man my mother will love, and then he will become my father, and then he will sacrifice his life for his beliefs. Even though I hated the Communists back then, I understood that my father had died believing that communism was the ideal solution for the poor, the workers, and the Jews.

My mother had told me that the name Jaworski belonged to a family of petty nobility that had lost all its money in the last century, so that several of its members had taken up farming and become little more than peasants. No doubt that was true enough as far as the actual Jaworskis were concerned.

I was four when my father died in prison — that is, when he was killed there. Soon after, there was a fire in our house and nothing at all was left. The two or three photographs that we had of my father went up in flames too. My mother had grabbed me in the nick of time and pulled me outside, although not fast enough to avoid a scar on her foot where she was burned. And yet though the prison and the fire were real, I couldn't visit my father's grave or light candles for him on All Souls' Day, because according to my mother the prison had donated his body to medical science. In those days medical students had such trouble finding cadavers that they sometimes paid a lot of money for them.

It upset me a lot when I was a boy that my father didn't have a grave. As if being an orphan with a stepfather wasn't bad enough, I didn't even have a father's grave to cry at! Before the war I had all kinds of answers for the children who asked me where my father was buried. When I was little I can remember telling them that he was buried in the tomb of the Unknown Soldier, which was why I had to be there for the changing of the guard. I really did go there often to see the ceremony. Sometimes I would dream of being in an old, neglected cemetery, not like the one in our churchyard that I was familiar with. Suddenly, burning on a grave, I saw candles like those lit on All Souls' Day. I approached closer and saw that the grave had a name and a date on it, but the more I tried to read them, the blurrier they became, until at last I saw nothing except for the candles still burning in the darkness.

When my father died, my mother went to 10 Nalewki Street, where his parents lived, and met his mother, my grandmother, for the first time. His father was no longer alive by then. My mother told my grandmother that my father was dead and that the prison had not returned his body, and the two of them embraced and cried in each other's arms.

I asked my mother how she got along with my father when it came to religion, because I knew that the Communists said there was no such thing as God. She answered that they found ways to compromise. In the end, she said, the Communists would be forced to make their peace with religion.

Whenever I found corroboration for one of her old stories about my father and herself, I breathed a sigh of relief. It was as if one more thing had been salvaged from my father's life, which had been left to me to resurrect. I was grateful for every little detail that could take the place of one of my fictions, so that I could stop patching and re-patching it. Like the story of how they met, for example.

They met at a May Day demonstration, because of a brawl. There were always brawls on May Day. It was the one day my mother used to lock me in the house and forbid me to go outside. But she liked to tell me how my father had rescued her from a fracas in which men were hitting each other with sticks and iron rods. Although the police, she told me, pretended to be breaking up the crowd and arresting the guilty parties, they would actually join the fray and help beat up the Reds.

She also told me about the conversations in her Communist cell. The cell had five members, two girls and three boys. When my father was tortured, he held out and didn't give them away.

Sometimes I lie in bed at night thinking of prisoners being tortured, not by the Gestapo, but by our own Polish government. I try to imagine all kinds of torments and wonder if I could hold out under them. I rather think that I could. I would simply scream and scream until I passed out from so much screaming. I would scream myself to death. And yet when I think about torture after actually hurting myself — breaking a fingernail, for example, or banging my head against something — I doubt that I could survive it. At such times I think of my father and shiver.

My mother told me that in her underground cell there were always arguments and discussions. Sometimes these went on all night long and her parents worried about where she was. The cell members called each other not "Pan" and "Pani" but rather "Comrade." They argued about how communism would come about. Was it all right to kill in order to make it come faster? Did the end justify the means? My mother said it didn't. That's why she was expelled from the party, because she refused to go against her feelings and deny her religion. But my father went on loving her, even though this greatly angered his cell members. At about that time he traveled to Russia to see communism with his own eyes. When he came back he admitted that life was not ideal there, but he stayed in the party and went on organizing. He and my mother weren't married in church, because he said he didn't believe in it. And yet he never said he didn't believe in God: that was something my mother was prepared to swear to. (I knew even then, of course, that the Jewish God was the same as the Christian one, although Jews didn't believe in Jesus and Mary.) He just didn't like churches, said my mother. He didn't like to see money made from God. It didn't matter whether it was made by priests or rabbis. He had no use for either.

I've always been moved by the fact that my father believed in making the world a better place and had the courage to get up and do something about it.

Perhaps he also believed that, if there were no more rich and no more poor and brotherhood among all people, there would be no more differences between him and my mother. It's hard for me to believe that he wasn't aware of those differences, even if he said they didn't matter.

My father's refusal to have a church wedding, my mother told me, had nothing to do with his being Jewish. No one even knew he was a Jew. It was just a matter of being against organized religion. And so they crossed the German border to Breslau and were married in a civil ceremony, which was something that Poland didn't have. They didn't tell any of my grandparents about it until I was born, when everyone found out. My father's parents disowned him and my mother's parents disowned her. They didn't know my father was Jewish, but a non-Catholic wedding was not a wedding for them, which meant that my mother was living in sin. Even after I was accepted as one of the family, my grandmother, my mother's mother, used to call me "the bastard" whenever she was mad at me.

My mother had me baptized as a Catholic without telling my father she was doing it, because she was afraid he wouldn't let her. When she told him about it later, though, he wasn't angry at all. He just laughed and said that had he known, he would have baptized me at home with tap water.

He was caught and put into prison in 1933. He was there for three months before he died. My mother kept a yellow piece of old newspaper with a story about some Communist who was shot to death during an attempted jailbreak.

4

Antony

Did Antony know I was half Jewish? And if he did, how could he still have wanted to adopt me? Perhaps, I thought hopefully, my mother had never told him. Otherwise it was beyond my powers of comprehension, because after the Germans, Antony hated Jews and Communists in that order. And even if the order was sometimes reversed, so that he hated Communists more than Jews, he was bringing up a boy whose father had been both.

Immediately after my mother told me about my father, I was so involved with myself and with figuring out who I was if my father had been a Jew that I forgot all about Antony. I was already in school when I began to consider his side of it. That gave me another jolt. All I could think about until the last bell was whether he knew or not. I tried to remember if my mother had ever dropped any clue. It seemed likely that she hadn't told him after all. Wasn't it enough for him to know that my father was a Communist? After a while I began to think that Antony couldn't possibly know. He would never have married the ex-wife of a man who was both a Communist *and* a Jew. Antony knowing Father was Jewish seemed out of the question, and I desperately wanted to believe that there was some logic involved. Gradually, though, the thought of my mother's honesty began to make me more and more anxious. Suppose she decided to tell Antony the truth now? I tried thinking of some magic formula that could convince her not to. And then I had an idea: even if Antony knew, as long as he didn't know that I knew, everything would stay the same, as if nothing at all had happened.

I hurried home and waited impatiently for my mother to arrive. I kept praying that she would get there before Antony, and I put the question right to her when she did.

He did know! And so I asked my mother, I begged her, not to tell him about my taking the Jew's money. I wasn't worried about the money itself, which didn't matter that much to me anyway. And I was sure that if Antony found out about it, he would never let my mother give it away, even if he punished me for taking it. Antony hated blackmailers like Pan Krol but he wasn't about to part with good money. I tried convincing my mother to leave things as they were, because as long as Antony didn't know that I knew, he could go on feeling the same toward me. It was bad enough that I would have to feel differently toward him.

I talked on and on. My mother listened and said nothing. At last, though, she agreed.

But I still had a problem with Antony. I couldn't hate him anymore the way I used to. Worse yet, I couldn't look down on him and feel superior.

Mostly, I hated Antony because of my mother. And I began to hate him more than ever when I found out what they did at night.

The son of some neighbors, a boy older than myself, took it upon himself to tell me. He explained it in great detail. I can remember us standing in the darkness of the stairwell and breaking off our conversation each time someone passed by. Finally his mother came out, because the neighbors had told her that we were up to something or perhaps smoking on the sly.

To this day I can see the glee in his eyes at the sight of my shock, hurt, and disbelief. I was just a small boy and he was a big one, and he kept laying it on me over and over: "Your father, he sticks it into —" Well, you know the rest. I thought he must be the biggest sinner in the world, and I was sure he would be struck down by lightning any minute.

But he wasn't. And so I started to argue with him. First of all, I said, it couldn't be true because it was a sin. He agreed with that. It was not only a sin, he told me, it was the original sin for which Christ had died to save the world. But it was the only way to make babies. You did it and then you went to the priest and were given a penance. I swore up and down that he was wrong about my mother. She and Antony would never do such a thing. The proof was that they had never had any babies. But all my logic didn't do any good.

Before the neighbors' son explained all this, I hadn't paid it any attention. Maybe it was because I played so much football and ran around so much in the street that I fell asleep as soon as my head hit the pillow. From that day on, though, I began to listen. After I heard them doing it once, I began to cover my ears with the pillows each time they started.

Later on, I went into the sex education business myself along with Wacek and Janek. The lessons I gave were just like the one I received.

But I didn't stop hating Antony.

Once I saw him shaving my mother's legs with his big razor. He was doing it for her because the razor scared her to death. To tell the truth, it scared me too. I think razor blades must have been invented by then, but Antony had no use for such children's toys. I stepped into the bathroom one night when they thought I was asleep and saw him doing it. And now, suddenly, I couldn't hate him as much as I liked anymore because he knew all about me. I was in a real dilemma. I think it was a turning point in my life, because for once it made me think and use my brain.

Until then I had enjoyed thinking of Antony as a kind of caveman, the last of a long line of garbage men, which was what his family had been for generations. Not to say that wasn't work that somebody had to do, but I never missed a chance to look down on him, even for his name.

I liked my mother's maiden name: Aniela Barbara Rejmont. Her father, my grandfather, was a relative of the famous Polish author Wladislaw Stanislaw Rejmont. But I couldn't stand Antony's family name, which she took as her own. It absolutely killed me each time I heard a neighbor or shopkeeper call her "Pani Skorupa" and I always blamed her for not keeping my father's name. She could have called herself Pani Jaworski-Skorupa had she wanted, or even Pani Rejmont-Jaworski-Skorupa.

My mother called Antony by his first name, although when she wanted to put him in his place she called him "Skorupa" or "Pan Skorupa." That would make him lose his temper and call her "Pani Rejmont," which was his way of saying, "Just get a load of the fine lady!"

He was a simple, uneducated man who had barely finished fourth grade and never read a book in his life. And yet my mother had married him, which was something I couldn't understand. I was five years old at the time and I remember going to church for the wedding.

It took a long time before I agreed to call him "Antony." Instead I called him "Pan Antony." I often eavesdropped on what he and my mother were saying in their room and once or twice I heard him trying to convince her to make me change. At first he insisted that I call him "Papa." Later he dropped this demand and began to talk about adoption instead. By then, though, I was much bigger, and when my mother broached the subject I ran away from home for three days to my grandparents'. I was sure my father would turn over in his grave if I agreed. Eventually Antony gave up, although now and then I heard him say to my mother that it was a disgrace for me to address him like a stranger when he had raised me from the age of five. It embarrassed him in front of the neighbors and in front of my teachers in school. What had he done to deserve it? But I went on calling him "Pan Antony," although whenever I could I avoided addressing him by name at all.

When I was smaller, before the war, I was sometimes fresh to him and called him names like "Stinker" because he smelled of sewage. Finally, I'm sorry to say, he spanked me so hard one day that my behind was red for a week. My mother was furious at him. She had never spanked me in my life. I remember him saying that if he were my natural father he would have taken his belt and whipped some sense into me, the same way it was whipped into him when he was a boy. Had he turned out any the worse because of it? But my mother forbade him to hit me again and made me promise never again to be fresh to him. Then she had a long talk with me.

She took me for a walk by the banks of the Wisla River. It was one of my favorite things to do with her, to walk by the river on a moonlit night. We would stroll slowly while I held her arm, and if it was winter she would wear her old fur coat that I loved to touch while, surrounded by silvery magic, we listened to the crunch of snow under our feet.

As we talked my mother explained to me how she had come to marry Antony.

She had gotten to know him while my father was in prison. In the summer he used to make the rounds outside the prison building, selling ice cream from a big box strapped to his shoulder to supplement his paycheck from the municipality. Whenever my mother left the prison and sat down on the sidewalk to cry, he came over to comfort her with a free ice cream. I may not be an objective judge, but you can see from the photographs I have of her how beautiful she was. It wasn't just a matter of beauty either, because there was something about her that made people feel warm and trusting. Even when Antony found out that her husband was a Communist, and later yet, that he was a Jew on whose account she was raising a child born out of wedlock, he didn't abandon her like everyone else. Of course, no one but Antony knew that my father was Jewish. Most people were very religious and couldn't forgive my mother for living in sin.

She was forgiven only when she married Antony. That's when I first met my mother's parents, my grandfather and my grandmother, as well as the rest of the family that came to the wedding. I was very excited, because all the children I knew had at least one grandparent and several uncles and aunts, and now I would have some too.

Walking along the Wisla that night I promised my mother that I would never be fresh to Antony again, and it was a promise that I kept. In my bed at night, though, I would think of all the swear words I wanted to curse him with, and sometimes I would even whisper them to myself. Afterward I would tell the priest about it in confession. That way at least one person knew what I thought of my stepfather. The priest made me say some Paternosters for a penance, but I didn't mind. I liked praying before going to sleep anyway. It kept the ghosts away.

Nevertheless, there were times when I had to call Antony by name in order to get what I wanted. Whenever I wanted money or something like that, for instance, I had to swallow my pride and call him "Antony." I hated the way he smiled to himself then, but I had no choice, because he was in charge of the money. I couldn't even buy candy or the smallest thing without asking him, because my mother refused to do it for me.

There was one other time when I used to call him "Antony": when he was drunk. He didn't know what was going on then anyway.

Antony had an agreement with my mother that he could get drunk in the tavern once a week, every Sunday evening. That is, he could go to the tavern on other nights too and come back stinking of vodka, but he couldn't get drunk. And I must say that he kept his word.

Like all proper Poles, we went to mass every Sunday morning. Antony would put on the good suit he had bought from Jews in the ghetto for a song, I would wear my Sunday best, also bought from Jews, and my mother would have on one of the pretty new dresses that Antony had bought her. He swore they weren't from Jews, but he was lying of course, and I think my mother must have known it. She herself refused to wear Jewish clothes — out of sympathy, I imagine. Maybe she couldn't help thinking of the woman who had worn the dress before and now was dead. And so Skorupa gave her his word of honor that he had bought the dresses at a discount store. She looked so lovely in them that she made herself believe him.

After church we went for dinner to my grandfather and grandmother's on Bridge Street. When we returned home, the caveman — that's how I thought of him in those days — changed out of his good suit to spare it too much wear and went off to Pan Korek's tavern. If he didn't return in time for the curfew, my mother sent me to bring him. After the Germans instituted a nightly curfew in Warsaw, that became my regular job.

Every Sunday evening my mother would wander nervously around the house, looking constantly at her watch. I wasn't allowed out in case she should need me, and if Antony didn't come back in time, I was sent off to the tavern. I actually liked going there on Sunday evenings. It was different from the other days of the week. I knew what those were like because I worked for Pan Korek as a waiter and a dishwasher — sometimes one and sometimes the other. I never worked in his tavern on Sundays, though. My mother didn't allow it, not just because of all the drunks there, but also because of the Sabbath.

Sometimes when I came to get Antony he was in a conscious state and let me drag him outside with the help of Pan Korek. Pan Korek knew my mother from before the war, when she wasn't yet married to Antony, and he always lent a hand. It was all a question of whether I could manage to hold Antony up in the street and keep him pointed toward home, because he kept trying to wander off into other streets and all kinds of houses and doorways that he saw or imagined were there. I had to make sure he didn't fall headfirst through an open door he didn't see or bang his head into a wall because he was sure there was a door there.

Worst of all were the nights when he was already under the table when I came for him. That's when Pan Korek had to give me the three-wheeler he kept in the back of the tavern in return for my solemn pledge to bring it back the next morning as soon as the curfew was over. That meant at 5 A.M. (Pan Korek needed the three-wheeler that early because he used it to transport merchandise.) He would cover it with a blanket and I would promise to keep Antony from puking on it and to return it in clean condition. That meant that I had to get up on Monday mornings long before school began. Wacek and Janek knew the reason for it, which was what made them laugh when they ran into me that day.

To tell you the truth, I never knew if I should pray to find Antony under the table or still on his two feet. If he was totally potted, Pan Korek could help me seat him on the three-wheeler and I usually had no trouble afterward. It was much worse if he started home under his own power, and then, just when it looked as if he were going to make it, collapsed in the street. Sometimes I managed to catch him in time and force him to stagger on. But sometimes I didn't and he would simply fall down and flounder around on the ground.

Pan Korek's tavern wasn't far from where we lived. Still, it was a bit of a walk, and if Antony fell halfway home I had to go back for the three-wheeler, pedal as fast as I could to where I had left him, and get him onto it by myself, not to mention the times I returned to find him in the gutter or with his pockets picked by some street gang. Once or twice the police were already dragging him off to the station house when I arrived.

The first time that happened I showed up at the last minute and it was all I could do to talk them out of arresting him. The second time the police already knew me and were waiting for me to come back. "What a father you have," said one of them pityingly. I had enough brains not to correct him. I think the story must have made the rounds of the police force, because when it happened again all but one of the policemen were different and yet they sized up the situation at once and even helped me load Antony onto the three-wheeler and gave me a friendly slap on the back.

Even though the police worked for the Germans, Antony defended them. He said they had no choice and that it was just their job. Nevertheless, the word *police* became so hated in Poland that today we call it the militia instead.

When I finally got Antony home, I would whistle for my mother to come downstairs and help me drag him up. She refused to ask Valenty the doorman to help because she thought it undignified. She was after all a Rejmont, even if that meant she had to haul some sozzled caveman up the stairs. But she was happier when I brought Antony back on his own feet, despite the off-color songs he would sing at the top of his voice. I myself kind of liked them. I didn't understand all of them, but they had lots of dirty words and funny parts, and something about them rang true. If he sang a song that I liked especially, I would turn to him and say, "Sing us another, Antony." Or else I would applaud and say, "Encore, Antony, encore!"

I don't think I was ever as embarrassed by him as my mother was. After all, I hadn't married him. He wasn't my father and all the neighbors knew it. And the drunker he was, the nicer he became. He would suddenly begin to laugh, whereas usually he had a gloomy look except when he was with my mother. That was the only time he would talk to me like a friend. Once, I remember, he made some remark about my mother's behind. We had already reached our building and she heard. She came downstairs, clapped her hands, and exclaimed, "Why, you ought to be ashamed!"

5

Pan Jozek

Ever since the day my mother found the money and told me the truth about my father, my Monday mornings were different. If I had to return the three-wheeler, I didn't roam the streets when I was finished but went to church instead. It became a regular custom. Usually I would pray to the Virgin Mary. Since the unheated church was icy cold, I would go back outside as soon as my bones began to freeze to look for some sausage or roasted-chestnut vendor over whose stove I could warm my hands while waiting for school to start.

On at least three such Monday mornings I saw the man who crossed himself backward. The second time I noticed that he entered the church not through the main door but via a side entrance, creeping in silently and sitting down. When I had watched him enough to be sure that he was really making the sign of the cross wrong, I decided to move to a seat from which I could see him come in without being seen myself. The proof that he was a Jew, I decided, would be that he wouldn't bother to cross himself if he thought he was alone. And indeed, he didn't. I began to suspect that he was being hidden by the priest. This wasn't our priest, of course. I may have forgotten to tell you, but the church in question was one near my school, not the one near our house.

Finally, when he came in one day and sat down, I rose and walked by him on my way out in order to get a good look at him.

He wasn't especially frightened-looking or pale. He looked like someone who is in a strange city and has taken time out to enter a church. He wore a light gray coat and held a gray hat in one hand, and despite his youthful appearance he could have been an engineer or a doctor. Before the war he would have been taken for a student. At first glance he could even have been one of those German-speaking Poles who called themselves *Volksdeutsch*. He certainly didn't look Jewish, although there was something about him that my mother would have called "gentle" and that might have made Wacek and Janek follow him a bit to see what he was up to.

I left the church. I was already out in the street when I realized that was how I would have wanted my father to look: the light, unusual eyes, the straight nose and high cheekbones that gave him that Slavic look, the sensitive lips, the friendly, reliable expression. Today I would call it the expression of a remarkably successful impersonator. And yet as perfect a mask as it was, it left a shadow of sadness on his face.

The next time, I decided, I would wait to see if he went out into the street when he left the church or into the priest's quarters. I knew my following him might frighten him off, but I was curious and by now he knew me anyway, having seen me in church three or four times. I thought I should tell him he was crossing himself wrong and maybe even give him the money, which was still in safekeeping with my mother. Of course, we could always have given it to the Jews who were hiding at my Uncle Wladislaw's, but they were so rich they didn't need it. Sometimes when I was walking in the street I was sure that a man or a woman coming toward me was a Jew. I had no idea how to approach them, though, or what to say to them if I did. Besides, I couldn't take the money to school every day on the chance that I might meet a Jew to give it to. And yet I was beginning to worry that Antony might find it and worm the story out of my mother. If that happened, it certainly wouldn't end up in Jewish hands.

The next time I saw him, however, the man simply vanished from the church. He must have felt I was watching him and slipped away or hid. I couldn't start looking for him, because that would have been overdoing it.

And then one day, he rose and went out into the street. He was carrying a leather briefcase. Until then the only thing he had held was his hat.

I remember that day well, because it had been snowing for a week. The snow came early that year, and it was a beautiful, clear winter morning with a blue sky and no wind. It must have been about three weeks before Christmas.

I ran after him. He noticed me and tried to disappear around a corner. I slowed down and pretended that I just happened to be heading in the same direction. Although I made sure to keep him in sight, I had no idea what to do. I hadn't the foggiest notion of how to offer him the money. Who in Warsaw, in December 1942, was going to admit that he was Jewish? And yet if he didn't learn to cross himself right, it might cost him his life. I thought of handing him a note and leaving him, but I couldn't stop to write one now. I kept tailing him. The streets were full of people, all hurrying about their business. Lots of children were on their way to school. Suddenly everyone began to run in our direction. From far up the street a human wave was frantically billowing toward us.

"It's a German dragnet!" someone shouted.

I took a few more steps, until he turned to run too, and then I turned and ran by his side. When we reached a back alley that was a private short cut of mine, I pulled at his sleeve and shouted, "This way, mister! We can cut through here."

He hesitated for a moment. I didn't blame him. No one but the neighbors who lived there knew that it was a passageway to a parallel street. To anyone else it looked like the dead-end entrance to a house that had been leveled in the German air raids. I knew about it only because I sometimes took it on my way to school.

We ducked into the alleyway and clambered over the ruins of the building. Then we crossed a hole in a fence made by the neighbors and climbed some steps. Beyond them the ground sloped sharply downhill. We jumped over a low wall and were in the street. The shouts of "Dragnet! Dragnet!" sounded far away now.

The man set out in a direction opposite that of my school. I walked alongside him. We didn't speak until finally he said, "Thank you."

"You cross yourself backwards, Pan," I told him. "I saw you in church. If you don't cross yourself right, you'll be caught."

He pretended not to understand me. He looked at me, thought for a second, and said, "That must be because I'm a leftie." He laughed. So did I.

We ducked into a doorway and made sure no one was looking, and I taught him the sign of the cross. That is, he knew it already, he just started it from the wrong side. Maybe it really had to do with his being left-handed. I remember that when I was little and couldn't tell left from right, I always had to cross myself to remember which hand was my right one.

"If I walk with you," I told him, "you can be sure no one will suspect you." I was proud of myself for saying it so naturally, without having to think twice about it.

"I was so sure no one could tell me apart," he said disappointedly.

"No one could. Not from the looks of you. Although there is something about you that I can't put my finger on. Still, I don't think I would follow you if I . . . if I were . . . out to shake you down, for example."

"And you aren't?"

"No."

"You mean you don't want to know where I'm going?"

"No."

We walked in silence for a while. I wanted to say goodbye and be off, because I had stuck to him long enough. But I still had to tell him about the money. I had thought a lot about how I would offer the money to a Jew once I had started a conversation with him. What I had decided in the end was to say that my father owed a debt of honor to some Jew who had been taken away by the Germans and that he had asked me to give the money to some other Jew who needed it. Of course, my Jew would probably ask why my father didn't give the money away himself, but I could always say it was because he had died in the meantime. It was just that I couldn't get the words out of my mouth now. I was trying to make myself say them when he said, "The problem is that I don't know where to go now."

I racked my brain thinking what to do. Should I suggest somewhere to him? But where? Perhaps this was the time to bring up the money. But the faster I tried to think, the slower my mind worked. Meanwhile he continued: "It's not that I don't have an emergency address. I was there this morning. But the people who lived there have gone away and the doorman started asking questions. He gave me a funny look, and my answers just made it worse. In any case, it's clear that they won't be back soon. I know them, and I'm sure they would have left me a message if they could have. Something must have gone wrong. If there had been a death in the family, the doorman would have told me. It must be something else. Jews aren't the only ones who disappear these days. And today I have to move out of the apartment where I've been staying."

"You mean the priest's place?"

He didn't answer.

"I've seen you in that church every Monday."

"Yes," he said. "Every Monday his sister comes from the village with a package of food for him. And she insists on arranging it for him in the pantry by herself . . . "

I didn't get it.

"That's where he's been hiding me during the day."

"And now he doesn't want to anymore? You've run out of money?"

"No, it isn't that. He hurt himself yesterday falling off a streetcar. His sister has come to stay with him until he's better. That means that in the meantime . . . but just who exactly are you that you want to know everything about me?"

"I'm just someone who thought you needed help," I answered. It was the truth.

We walked on without speaking until he said abruptly, "I don't know many people in this city who go around helping Jews. Certainly not boys your age." I had to think of something quickly, so I said the first thing that came to mind: "My best friend was a Jewish boy. He was our neighbor. My mother and my stepfather were friends of his family." (Antony would have had a heart attack if he heard me saying that!) "Until they had to move to the ghetto. I'll bet they were killed there."

"What was his name?"

"Bolek," I said racking my brain for a Jewish last name. "Bolek Rosentsveig." I sighed.

Suddenly it dawned on me what we had done, what *I* had done, to the Jew whose money we took. He had been in the same kind of fix. I felt a twinge in my heart. What kind of person was I? I wondered. I had been so eager to get my hands on the money that I never stopped to think what I was doing. Was I really no different from my Uncle Wladislaw, who cared only about money? Or some gangster in America like the ones we saw in the movies? And apart from giving away the money, I couldn't think of any penance to make up for it. Everything else was either too harsh or too lenient — like not going to the movies, for instance. I wasn't supposed to go to them anyway, because my mother didn't allow me to watch the German propaganda that was shown there, but I wanted so badly to see some action on the screen that I didn't care what it was, as long as it was a film with things happening in it. Still, it was ridiculous to think you could make up for a human life by not going to the movies.

"Don't you have any other addresses?" I asked.

He did. Two others. The first, he said, belonged to

people who were undependable and he preferred not to risk it unless there was no choice. The second he was saving for a real emergency. The people who lived there, he explained, had neighbors who were informers. He loved them too much to endanger their whole family unless he absolutely had to.

We walked on in silence again until I asked, "So you need a place to stay in, is that it?"

"Yes," he said. "I have the money to pay for it. Although," he quickly added, "I don't have it with me right now."

"I have an uncle who hides Jews," I said. "If you'd like, I can ask him if he has room."

I hoped he would say yes.

"When can you do it?"

"Right now."

"How come you have a school bag but aren't in school?"

I was about to tell him that I had been sent home for one reason or another when I remembered that we had been together since early that morning, before school even began.

"I decided to play hooky," I said. "I hate school."

"And that's where you go to play hooky, to church?"

"I had lots of time, so I thought I'd go to confession."

"Are you such a big sinner?" he asked in an amused tone.

"Everyone's always got a sin or two," I said. "And sometimes I just feel like confessing."

"You know what? Go talk to your uncle. I don't have much to lose."

"Should we arrange to meet somewhere?" I asked.

"Why don't you suggest a place."

The only place I could think of was our church. I gave him the address and told him there was a little park there by the graveyard with some benches in it. He could make believe he was visiting the grave of a friend or something.

"All right," he said. "And if I'm ever in church again, I'll cross myself properly."

He grinned and so did I.

He was a really nice man. I had never thought that a Jew could be so like a Pole. That is, I had never thought about it until I found out about my father. My mother always said that all people looked alike when they smiled. When I was a little boy I used to think that might be true of everyone except the Jews, the ones with the beards on Nalewki Street, I mean. But when I started working with Antony and met the three brothers who bought food from him, I saw that they also smiled the same as everyone even though they were religious Jews with beards and sidelocks.

We said goodbye. He turned and walked back toward the church, and I went to my uncle's house on Zelazna Street. I took the streetcar to save time. I hoped that after hearing my story my mother would give me a note for school saying I was sick or something. Anything to keep my stepfather from finding out.

No one was in at my uncle's. That is, the Jews were

there all right, but they had to pretend that they weren't. They couldn't even flush the toilet in the bathroom. If they had to go somewhere in the apartment, they did it with their shoes off, and my uncle had marked the squeaky floorboards to keep them from stepping on them. They didn't open doors either, because they might creak, or turn faucets, because the pipes might rumble. My stepfather said that happened when there was air in them, but I never understood what air he was talking about. I only knocked once, so as not to frighten them.

I decided to bring the Jew to my grandparents' house in the meantime. My aunt and uncle were sure to return by the afternoon, so that I could get him out of there again before my grandmother came home from Theater Square.

My grandparents lived on Bridge Street, in the same building they had occupied before the war. We also still lived in the same building, but theirs had been leveled by the 1939 air raids and all that was left of it was a part of their apartment that had been beneath street level. Even that had not escaped damage: the plaster had fallen off the walls and there were cracks in them and in the ceiling. The one ground-floor room had been thoroughly demolished along with nearly all of their furniture, because it had served as the living room. I still remember everything that was in it, because I liked visiting my grandparents. It was an experience that never lost its newness after all the years in which my grandparents had broken off all contact with my mother.

Now, however, Grandfather was no longer the man he once was. A year after the war broke out he had gone "off his rocker" and begun to lose touch with reality. Sometimes he didn't know his own name or thought that I was his youngest son, my Uncle Romek. "Romek," he would ask me, "why didn't you buy me the newspaper?" I never knew whether to pretend that I really was my Uncle Romek or not. Or else he might say, "Romek, how come you're back from school in the middle of the week?" That annoyed him, because Romek had been sent to a military school.

Sometimes he had no idea who I was or what I was doing in his house. That rarely happened, though. Generally he realized I was a member of the family, even if he wasn't sure just which or from when. And he almost always recognized my mother, and of course, my grandmother too. He died about half a year after these events. He just went to sleep one night and never woke up.

Before the war my grandfather was a highly respected businessman who owned a print shop and was the father of four children who were raised by Grandmother: my mother, my Uncle Romek, my Uncle Wladislaw, and a little girl who died of pneumonia in childhood. My Uncle Romek was dead too. He was killed at the beginning of the war in the famous Polish cavalry charge against a German tank division.

Now, because of his condition, my grandfather was always at home, while my grandmother sold cigarettes and things in Theater Square. I could never have told her that I was bringing a Jew to her house, not even for only a few hours. Grandmother thought that all Jews were Devil worshipers, or at least, the Devil's assistants. I wonder what she would have said had she known the truth about my father, because she was actually very fond of me.

She was a country girl, not a city lady. My grandfather's family was furious at him for marrying an "uncouth peasant." But Grandmother was far from uncouth. She may never have read Shakespeare or learned to play the piano, but she had a good head on her shoulders. I've already said that Grandfather was a Rejmont, which is something I'm proud of to this day.

Every morning Grandmother dressed Grandfather and sat him down by the glass-paneled door, which also doubled as the window. If it wasn't winter and the weather was good, she would leave the door open, and if it was hot, she would seat him outside on a metal chair that was chained and padlocked to a water pipe to keep it from being stolen. Fortunately, Grandfather was still able to go to the bathroom by himself. Grandmother had sworn never to put him in a hospital ward or in an old-age home run by the church. They had been wed, she said, for good and for bad, and if now was the bad part, there had been many good years before that, when the world had still been a sane place. Which it had stopped being, Grandmother was convinced, because of all the Jewish inventions, like automobiles that flew through the air and dropped bombs.

One thing my grandfather could do to his dying day was roll cigarettes. He would make them at home and Grandmother would sell them in the square. She did something else there too that I wasn't supposed to know about: as innocent as she looked, she transmitted messages for the Polish Home Army. Someone would come along and tell her something, or hand her a note wrapped in a bill he had bought his cigarettes with, and she in turn would hand it to another customer with his change.

I often helped them roll the cigarettes. They used a copper tube slightly longer than two cigarettes which opened lengthwise on a hinge in such a way that it resembled two little drainpipes, which were filled with tobacco. You had to have a sense for how much to pack the tube, because if you crammed it with too much tobacco the cigarette paper tore, and if you used too little all the tobacco spilled out.

I think the underground chose my grandmother for several reasons. One was that she was already a street peddler anyway. Another was that she lived alone with her husband in a ruined building that had no doorman. Both were good reasons for me to think that I could safely leave the Jew in her house for several hours.

Afterward I found out that his first name was Jozek. He never told me his family name.

As soon as I reached Theater Square I spotted my grandmother in the distance. She was reaching for something in one of her skirt pockets — no doubt her twenty-zloty German cigarettes. She sold different brands and kept each one in a different place, wrapped in rags that she stuffed in the many pockets of her skirts and in my grandfather's old jacket that she wore. She wore one skirt over another, just like the peasants in the countryside.

"Good morning, Grandma," I said to her.

The customer departed.

"What's this, no school today?"

I told her I was sent home for not doing my homework. It wasn't such a big lie, because I really hadn't done it.

She believed me. "Come, sit down with your old Grandma for a while," she said.

"I can't," I said. "I was just passing by and decided to say hello to you."

She believed that less. "Would you take something to Grandpa for me?"

I said I would. She took a flat can from one of her pockets and told me I could have some of it too.

"What is it?"

"Can't you read? Read it!"

I read it. Sardines. She shook a finger at me.

"I said you could have *some,* not all of it. Don't forget. Grandpa may not remember if he ate sardines or not, but I'll find out the truth."

She was just like my mother that way: she always knew when I was lying. The difference was that she would slap me for doing it.

My mother told me that Grandfather used to whip his sons with a belt. He would lay them across his knees and let them have it. The older the son, the harder the whipping. Grandmother educated my mother with slaps, but it was the-older-the-harder with her too, until one day my mother said that she was a woman already, and the slapping stopped. I wasn't sure what she meant by that. She always said she would explain it to me some day, but she never did.

"Bye, Grandma," I said, giving her a kiss.

That was a mistake. She knew right away that I was up to something because of the kiss. I really shouldn't have given it to her. I was just so happy to have found her there and to have a place to put Pan Jozek.

"I have no money to waste on you," she said. "Get along with you, you young scamp!"

"It was just a kiss," I said. "I didn't mean anything by it."

When she got home, I thought, we would already be gone. And my grandfather would be in his usual fog. You know, I believe in God. Even then I believed that God arranges things so that we can choose between good and evil. The whole point is to choose.

6

Marek Wins Over Pan Jozek

It was a very old graveyard. Many of the graves had dates centuries old. As a little boy before the war, I remember, I sometimes used to run out to it when I grew tired of sitting quietly in church on Sunday morning. I know that most children are afraid of cemeteries. I never was, though. More than anything I wanted my father to have a grave we could visit. Maybe that's why I invented a game. Since I thought that people who died could get together afterward like children during recess in school, I would walk between the rows looking for a grave with a name on it I liked, which I would decide must belong to a friend of my father's in the next world.

Pan Jozek wasn't in the park. I thought that maybe he had entered the church, but he wasn't there either. That meant, I supposed, that he hadn't trusted me enough to keep our rendezvous. Agreeing to meet me was just a way to throw me off his trail. Although I didn't blame him, I really did feel sorry. I walked through the park again, checking all the corner benches by the fence, and went back out to the street. Could he have waited for me and given up? Or maybe something had happened to him . . . Well, it wasn't my fault that my aunt and uncle weren't home. I debated whether to take a streetcar back to my grandmother's or to walk. Though I no longer hitched rides on the back of streetcars, I had a little money with me. My mother had caught me hitching a ride once and had made me promise to stop.

I fingered the can of sardines in my pockets. I felt like having something to eat. I was trying to think of the nearest streetcar I could take when I saw Pan Jozek step out of a bookstore with two books under his arm. And a newspaper. When I came closer, I saw that it was a German one. I noticed that one of the books was in German too. It hadn't been a bad place to stay out of sight while waiting for me. He knew he would see me, because he had a clear view of the street through the store window.

"Hello there," I said, as if we were old friends.

He went along with it, even though the street was nearly empty. "Why, hello there! How are you?"

I hadn't told him my name yet.

We could have passed for an elder and a younger brother, or for neighbors. Or else, he could have been my teacher. But no, he couldn't have been, not at that hour of the morning.

"Did you give up on me?"

He nodded. "It took you a long time."

"No one was home at my uncle's," I said. "But we can go wait at my grandfather's. They must have gone out shopping or on some business. They always come back before noon."

I told him that from my uncle's I had gone to Theater Square to make sure that my grandmother was there and hadn't stayed home with my grandfather. I told him about Grandfather and explained that the building had no doorman because it wasn't a building anymore. Then I showed him the can of sardines.

Right away someone came up to me and asked if I was selling. I said I wasn't. He insisted on knowing how much I wanted for the sardines. I repeated that they weren't for sale. He looked suspiciously at Pan Jozek and said, "I'll top any offer he makes you."

I thought it over, but I still didn't sell. When he was gone I asked Pan Jozek if he would come and wait with me in my grandparents' apartment until noon. He agreed.

"Now you look like a student, or even like Volksdeutsch," I said to him.

That pleased him so that he stretched out his arms as though giving the world a hug and said, "My, what a beautiful day!"

I too loved those winter days with a suddenly blue sky and snow glittering all around. There wasn't a breath of wind. The air was so fresh and pure that you felt you had never been so alive. I had known all morning that it would turn out to be a beautiful day, but Pan Jozek said it so feelingly that I thought he might dance in the street.

I thought of all the months he had been holed up in the priest's pantry. "Where's your family?" I asked.

"They've all been killed except for my mother. She managed to escape the Germans' clutches."

"How?" I asked.

"By dying first."

As I walked by his side I kept looking all around me, not the way I usually did but through Pan Jozek's eyes. I tried seeing everything for the first time: the snow-covered park, the newspaper vendors, the peasant women peddling food from baskets, the mothers out for a stroll in the sun with their baby carriages.

"Suppose your mother were still alive," I said. "What would you have done?"

"Are you asking me if I would have left the ghetto without her? No, I wouldn't have. As a matter of fact, we could have left long ago, before the deportations began. The Germans call them 'resettlement' — that means they resettle us in the world to come. There was a village family that was willing to hide both of us. But my mother refused to go because she couldn't keep kosher there. Do you know what that is?"

I didn't. He explained it to me.

I remember thinking: the poor Jews, as if being Jewish weren't hard enough, they have all these laws to make it even harder! The only Jewish law I had known before was the one about not eating pork. Some boys in school told everyone how the Germans caught Jews and forced them to eat it. There was one little boy there who said, "Then I'll make believe I'm a Jew and they'll make me eat it too." He had to have it explained to him that he didn't wear a hat or grow a beard like a Jew and that once he ate the pork he'd be killed.

"You can't even see the Wisla from the ghetto," Pan Jozek said.

That was something I had never thought of when picturing the ghetto. I couldn't imagine life without the Wisla. What would I do in the summer if I couldn't sit by its banks and watch the ships passing by? I'd go out of my mind, that's what. During summer vacations I used to work in Pan Mueller's boat-rental house. Sometimes, when business was slow, he would let me go for a row and dive off the boat as much as I pleased. And he would even pay me for it! Of course, he sometimes hit me too.

"How old are you?"

"Fourteen. I keep my birth certificate in my pocket so that the Germans won't draft me into a work gang. I've carried it around ever since they almost did that because they thought I was older."

"I also thought you were at least sixteen. How come they let you go?"

"There was a policeman who recognized me from Pan Korek's tavern. I work there sometimes too."

I told him about the tavern on Grzybowska Street and what I had to do there.

"I really was a student before the war," he told me. "Of medicine."

"Then you know what a doctor does?"

"Not quite. Why do you ask?"

"Because of my grandfather," I said.

But that wasn't really it. I had always wanted to know a doctor, not the way you know one when you see him in his office with a lot of people waiting outside, including your mother, but the way you know a friend. I could have asked him about all kinds of things that my parents and the priest said were a sin. Like masturbation. But of course, I didn't tell Pan Jozek all that.

He stopped to buy cigarettes and matches from the lame lady I always passed on my way to my grandparents'. Suddenly he pointed to a house and said, "That's where we lived in the ghetto."

I had completely forgotten that as recently as the previous summer the area we were walking in had been the Little Ghetto. My aunt and uncle lived in an apartment at 62 Zelazna Street, near the old Akron Movie Theater, which had belonged to Jews. They even gave me some toys they found when they moved in. They took me into a room that had two big light-blue shelves full of books and playthings and told me to take what I wanted. Some of them were broken. There were two beds that must have belonged to two brothers, because I didn't see any girls' toys, except maybe the three teddy bears and a monkey that I didn't take. But they could have belonged to a small boy too. I was surprised that the books were regular Polish ones, and that the toys were just like the ones that Polish children played with. There wasn't anything in Jewish letters or particularly Jewish looking.

That, by the way, was where I found *Les Misérables*.

Children's rooms with two beds in them always made me jealous. I always wanted a little brother or sister. I just didn't want one who was Antony's child.

On the way to Bridge Street Pan Jozek decided to turn right and walk through Old Warsaw. That was a part of the city I liked to walk in too. When I visited my grandparents, I sometimes went out of my way to pass through it.

We crossed the Wisla on the Kerbedzia Bridge and stood in the middle of it looking down on the river. Here and there you could already see ice against the banks. The tour boats, rowboats, and kayaks were gone, but it was such a nice day that despite the snow and bare trees you expected a boat to come sailing beneath the bridge any minute.

What did come by as we stood there were two barges loaded with lumber. I liked looking down at the flowing water. Pan Jozek put it well when he said that it was just as hypnotic as fire. He asked me, "Have you ever been to the seashore?"

I never had. It was a long way from Warsaw, although my mother had promised we would go there after the war. I tried to imagine the Wisla without its opposite bank, the way it was on a foggy day. Was that what the ocean looked like?

I asked Pan Jozek. He said that it wasn't. I remember him saying, "A river is a river and an ocean is an ocean. Each has its own beauty, its own sound, its own smell. I love the ocean and I love the Wisla too."

I was struck by what he said because until then I had never thought that a Jew could love the Wisla the way I did.

As we came off the bridge, he asked me what my name was. I told him and explained about my mother's family name and about Antony's. He said that his first name was Jozek, and that I should call him "Pan Jozek." To this day I don't know why he never told me his last name.

My grandfather was sitting behind the closed door as he always did in cold weather, looking out the glass pane that my grandmother had scraped the frost off before leaving. I never could tell what he saw. Sometimes, when I approached from the street, it seemed to me that he wasn't seeing anything even though his eyes were wide open. He always sat with his walking stick, which he tapped so often on the wooden floor that there was a hollow in the floorboard. Sometimes he drew on the glass door with his finger. His lower jaw hung open and made him look a hundred years old, because Grandmother kept his false teeth locked in the closet.

He didn't notice us come in because he was talking to someone in low tones.

Grandfather generally liked to talk to either his older sister or one of his parents. If he was arguing, that meant it was his sister. His tone with his mother was more conversational. I tried to make out what he was saying to her, but it was impossible. Now and then a sentence would make sense, followed by many that didn't. For instance, I once heard him say, "Mama, those cigarettes could be sold for good money, but that bastard of a German didn't flush the toilet." Different stories or memories must have combined with each other in some part of his brain.

When he spoke to his father, he always called him sir. Some Polish children "sir" their father to this day.

"Good morning, Grandpa!" I shouted, because he was a little deaf in the bargain. He stood up at once, though, when I showed him the can of sardines.

"They're from Grandma," I said.

We helped him hobble to the table and sat him down there. I was afraid the house would be cold, because my grandmother usually saved the wood for the evening, but some embers were still burning in the oven and the apartment was cozy. My grandfather didn't pay Pan Jozek any attention. He seemed to take it for granted that he was my guest. Pan Jozek took off his coat and I hung it with his hat on a hanger. When Antony was being nasty about Jews, one of the things he said was that they never took their hats off in their houses. I didn't believe him, though. It was true that the three brothers kept their hats on, but that was down in the basement. I couldn't imagine anyone coming into his own home, or entering someone else's, and not taking off his hat. I was sure it was one of Antony's anti-Semitic inventions.

I took half a loaf of bread and a wedge of cheese

from the pantry and put out three mugs and some clabber that my grandmother had made by warming milk near the oven till it soured. Then I set the table with plates and silverware. We didn't have guests or sardines every day! I filled the kettle and put it up to boil, adding some wood to the fire. My grandparents had neither gas nor electricity. At night they sat by candlelight or lamplight. My grandmother said she didn't want any inspectors reading meters or collecting bills. Looking back on it today, I think it was less a matter of her being stingy than of her being in the underground.

Grandfather wanted to slice the bread himself, but his hands shook too hard. And so he just crossed himself and said the Lord's blessing while I took the key to the little closet from its hiding place and brought him his false teeth. Then we sat down to eat.

It was only then that I realized how hungry Pan Jozek was. Between one bite and the next he wanted to know why the teeth were kept under lock and key. I told him that Grandfather sometimes lay down and fell asleep, and that if he swallowed the teeth he could choke. Or else, if he took them out of his mouth to play with while sitting in his chair by the door, they might fall and break.

Suddenly Grandfather stopped eating and froze with his fork halfway to his mouth. I had hoped he wouldn't do that and embarrass me, because he sometimes forgot that he was eating and would just sit there holding his spoon or fork until his food spilled on the floor. I took the fork from his hand and fed him.

"You take good care of your grandfather," said Pan Jozek.

"I guess I'm used to it," I said. Maybe I shouldn't have added what I did, but I couldn't resist. I laughed and said, "If my grandmother knew that a Jew sat here at her table, she'd scrub it down with disinfectant."

"Does she hate Jews that much?"

"Yes," I said.

"Does your whole family?"

"Not all of it. I don't know about my uncle who was killed. My Uncle Wladislaw doesn't love Jews, but he doesn't hate them either. He just makes money off of them. Not from blackmail or informing." I swallowed hard. "From hiding them. That's the uncle I went to see this morning."

"And your mother?"

"My mother believes that everyone is equal before God. It doesn't matter what you believe, or what you wear or eat. Whatever my grandmother says, she always says the opposite."

"And your stepfather?"

I told him.

"It's just that he hates the Germans even more. And maybe the Communists too. He says that if it weren't for the Germans, we'd have to get rid of the Jews by ourselves. He thinks we should send them all to Palestine. He's even willing to pay for it. He thinks that Poland has room for only one people."

"But what about the Byelorussians and Ukrainians who live in Poland too?"

I shrugged. The subject had never come up. "Anyway you look at it, they're Christians and not Jews," I said.

"They still don't consider themselves Poles," said Pan Jozek. He asked me what Grandfather thought.

"Grandpa!" I shouted. "What do you think of the Jews?"

I didn't think he'd understand me. After reflecting for a minute, though, he declared solemnly, "The Jews — lice — typhoid fever!"

I was amazed that he remembered the German notices he had read. Sometimes he surprised me by being more together than I thought.

"Are you still hungry, Pan Jozek?" I asked.

"What else is there to eat?"

There were eggs. While the water boiled in the kettle, I fried some up. I even ate one myself. By now I was full, but watching Pan Jozek eat gave me a new appetite. Then I made Grandfather a scrambled egg and fed him. He liked scrambled eggs. He could eat them even without his teeth. I thought it a good time to take them out of his mouth, but he wouldn't let me have them. All right, I thought, I'll do it when we're finished.

Afterward we drank tea like Grandfather and Grandmother. Actually, my mother and Antony drank it that way too. You bite off a piece of a sugar cube, put it under your tongue, and sip your tea through it, which makes it very sweet. It wasn't a question of saving sugar, though maybe that's how it started. It was simply the way my family drank tea. Now I saw that it was Pan Jozek's way too.

That was when Grandfather began to make a scene. He didn't want to give me his teeth back. I tried to convince him, and so did Pan Jozek. But Grandfather just shut his mouth tight and turned his back on us. He even shut his eyes and pretended not to hear.

Pan Jozek thought that as long as someone was with him, we could let him keep his teeth. And so I told him to stay put and wait for me while I went to talk to my mother. It had suddenly occurred to me that it would be better for her to speak to my aunt and uncle.

My mother was the only person who knew what I had done, and I was sure she would understand and help me to persuade my uncle. Pan Jozek, however, I now discovered, put no stock in my plans.

"It's been a pleasure, Marek," he said. "Maybe it was because we were both running from the Germans when we met, or because I saw that you weren't trying to blackmail me, or because I already knew you from the church, but for a while I really thought that going to your uncle's was a good idea. It was such a beautiful day that I couldn't resist running the risk of putting my faith in you. The more I think about it now away from the pressure of the street, though, the less logical it seems. I wanted to tell you that before, but I put it off because it seemed harmless to sit for a while in your grandfather's house while I thought of what to do next."

"What will you do?"

"First, I'll try the worse of the two addresses."

"But why? Why not try me? I'll go talk to my mother and everything will be all right. There's no problem about my uncle taking Jews."

"Suppose I agreed: what would you tell your mother? That you met a Jew in the street and want your uncle to take him in?"

I shook my head.

"Then what? Do you expect her to take the responsibility on herself? Usually, anyone hiding Jews gets them from a reliable source. Your uncle might think I was a blackmailer myself, or a double agent working for the Germans. And forgive me for saying so, but I can't help thinking that there's something strange about this whole business. Why on earth are you going to so much trouble to help me?"

I didn't know how to answer.

"Suppose your mother talks it over with your stepfather, and he goes and calls the police? Or your grandmother comes home while you're not here and takes me for a burglar? It's all much too risky for me." He rose to go.

"My grandmother never comes home before late afternoon," I said on the verge of despair.

But he had stopped taking me seriously. "Anyway, Marek, thanks an awful lot. At least I ate well. That priest who hid me begrudged me every slice of bread." He smiled.

Holy Mother of God, I wanted him to stay in the worst way! That's when I decided to tell him the truth. At least some of it. I asked him to sit down again for a minute, because I had something to say to him. He sat down and looked at me curiously. I told him how I had been walking up Grzybowska Street early one morning when I ran into Wacek and Janek, and how, although I sometimes went along with them, I had never gone Jew hunting before, and how I did it this time because I was sure that they would do it anyway without me, and how I couldn't resist having all that money to throw around, and how my mother had caught me red-handed. Finally, I told him that my mother still had the money, and that I wanted to give it to him, or at least to pay for his expenses while it lasted.

I don't think I ever talked so much in my life. I went on and on until I had nothing left to say while he sat there thinking and Grandfather tapped his finger on the table: tak tak stop and tak tak stop again.

"And you really think your mother will be willing to take the responsibility for your uncle taking me in?"

I shrugged.

"All right," he said. "Let's give it a try."

7

Grandfather's Teeth and Pan Korek

I was just in time to catch the number fifteen streetcar to Wilson Square. From there I walked to the sewing shop where my mother worked as a seamstress. I told her I had been bad in school and was sent home to bring her to the principal. Her Volksdeutsch boss laughed and wagged a finger at me when she asked him for permission to leave work, but he let her off. As soon as we had left I told her everything, starting with my noticing Pan Jozek in church and our slipping through the German dragnet, which made her ask if I had my birth certificate in my pocket. "You were lucky," she said when I told her we had gone to my grandparents' because my uncle and aunt weren't home. She wanted to hear everything Pan Jozek and I had talked about, and she hugged and kissed me when I was finished. That made me feel better already. "The first thing to do," said my mother, "is to go see that priest."

We took a bus to the church and knocked on the door of the priest's quarters. An old hag opened the door and told us we couldn't come in. "My brother has had a bad accident and isn't seeing anyone," she said sharply while slamming the door in our face.

We didn't give up. We knocked and knocked until we heard the priest's voice telling his sister to let the good Catholics in. She opened the door again, but only for my mother. I was told to wait outside.

It took a while for my mother to come back out, because at first the priest denied everything, even though she whispered her questions in his ear to keep his sister from hearing. In the end he had to send her out to buy him cigarettes and a newspaper. She understood of course that he was trying to get rid of her and stormed out the door muttering about her brother's ingratitude and something else that I couldn't make out. A few minutes later my mother emerged and told me that everything was all right. The priest had given Pan Jozek a clean bill of health.

From there we went to my uncle and aunt's on Zelazna Street. You had to enter a courtyard to reach their apartment, but the gatekeeper knew us. They were both home. Once again I had to wait in a hallway. Then I was called inside, where my uncle gave me a look that frightened me a bit. All he said, though, was that he had no room. If the back room became available, he would keep it for my Jew — provided, of course, that he was still alive and hadn't found another place. Meanwhile, he advised us to try Pan Korek, who was sure to take the Jew for less money. Pan Jozek wouldn't be as safe there as he would be at my uncle's, but my uncle was simply full up. In any case, Uncle Wladislaw said, we should keep all the money so that we could give him a big advance if we brought the Jew.

My mother answered that she wasn't going to pay a penny more than she had said she would. A month's advance was the maximum. And no deposit, either. She had never heard of a brother asking his sister for such a thing!

I realized at once that it was a mistake for her to have told my uncle about the money. The problem was that otherwise she couldn't have told him the truth — and my mother, as I've said, hated to lie, especially to the members of her family. Besides which, she was no doubt right in thinking that nothing but the truth could convince Uncle Wladislaw to take Pan Jozek at all. Still, she couldn't restrain herself from saying with a hard look at my uncle, "Pan Korek gives all the money he gets for hiding Jews to the underground."

"To each his own," said my uncle.

We left. My mother was furious. She started to say that my uncle was as money-mad as a J — but felt too uncomfortable to say the word. And she really wasn't anti-Semitic. It was just an expression people used.

It astounded me to find out that Pan Korek hid Jews. I would never have guessed it, though I worked several days a week in his tavern. True, I had never been up to the apartment above it, but you would have thought that I'd notice something. He must have gone up there to tend to things only after hours. I was sure he would take in Pan Jozek if we asked him.

We went to his tavern. It wasn't far away. I asked

my mother not to tell Pan Korek the whole truth. She should just say that she knew Pan Jozek, or better yet, his father. Something of the sort.

She promised to think of something and tołd me not to worry.

I was worried anyway about what we would do if Pan Korek wasn't there. And my mother would be so late in getting back to work that her boss might begin to suspect something.

I liked coming to the tavern at an hour when it was empty but already spick-and-span for opening time. It was quiet and cozy inside, and didn't stink of cigarette smoke, cheap cigars, and the homemade potato liquor everyone called *bimber*.

Pan Korek was in his office. He was an incredibly big man. My mother said that he reminded her of my father. She told me that the two of them were friends before my father became a Communist. Later, when my father came back from Russia, their relationship cooled a bit. Pan Korek was never against religion and never thought that it was the opium of the people.

Sometimes I asked my mother if she thought that I too would have fought with my father because of his views. She was sure that I would have. Back then, during the war, I had unthinkingly absorbed Antony's opinions. My father would never have stood for them, although my mother was sure he would have lost all his pro-Russian illusions after the pact between Hitler and Stalin that divided up Poland between them. My mother thought that Hitler's attacking Russia was the Russians' punishment for having betrayed us. It was like betraying your own brother, she said. But she thought the Russians would save us in the end and pay back their debt to us. If Antony were around at that point, he would be sure to add, "Sure thing! The old Russian bear hug. Good for a hundred years!"

My mother closeted herself with Pan Korek for ten long minutes while I wondered if she would keep her promise and not involve me.

When they stepped out of his office, Pan Korek said, "Your mother vouches for a young Jew whose father was a friend of Broneslaw's. She's ready to pay an advance for him. That's good, because we need the money." Pan Korek knew that I knew he was in the underground.

At this point I should explain: the People's Army and the Polish Home Army were the two main anti-German resistance movements. The first were "reds" and Communists; the second were "greens" and Catholics. Antony thought that the Home Army were patriots and that the People's Army were Bolshevik traitors. Even though it fought the Germans, the Home Army had a reputation for hating Jews. It refused to give them shelter or accept them as partisans, and was even said to turn them over to the Germans. I don't mean to say that every member of the Home Army was anti-Semitic, but there were plenty who were. And of course, not everyone in the People's Army loved Jews either. On the whole, though, they treated Jews well.

The two armies were a subject that Antony and my mother were no more able to agree on than they were able to agree about the Jews. My mother and Pan Korek were for the People's Army, whereas Antony, my grandmother, and I were for the Home Army. That wasn't what made me take the Jew's money, though. When it came to Jews as people, my views were like my mother's. All I agreed with Antony and my grandmother about was that there were too many Jews in Poland and that they should go to Palestine.

My mother and I left the tavern. She had kept my secret. I should be sure to tell Pan Jozek, she instructed me, of the "friendship" between his father and my grandfather. She had told Pan Korek that the two of them were both interested in old books, and that my grandfather had bought rare items for his library from Pan Jozek's father. After a moment's hesitation she told me where the money was hidden and how much I should pay Pan Korek, because she herself had to hurry back to work. I felt proud to be trusted with it.

"How much should we put aside for Uncle Wladislaw?" I asked her.

That made her angry all over again. "Don't worry," she said, "there's enough. But Pan Jozek can stay with Pan Korek. We won't have to bring him to my brother's."

My mother gave me change to take the streetcar home and get some money for Pan Korek. At first I thought I'd leave my school bag at home, but then I changed my mind. I had started thinking like a member of the underground — and a boy with a school bag would look less suspicious if he were accompanying Pan Jozek all the way from my grandparents' to the tavern.

By the time I reached Bridge Street I was beginning to worry that Pan Jozek might not be there anymore. But he was. He was sitting by the table, reading Grandfather the newspaper, or rather, translating for him from the German. I told him about Pan Korek and said that my uncle might have a place for him at a later date if he was still interested. I didn't tell him that my uncle was money-mad. Whatever I thought of him, he was my mother's brother and I had to protect the family honor.

Pan Jozek said that my mother's story wasn't that far from the truth, because his father had actually been a used-book dealer back before the First World War. He had already put on his coat and taken his hat when we suddenly remembered Grandfather's teeth. We couldn't leave them in his mouth, and Grandfather, for some odd reason, refused to let us have them. Perhaps he just didn't want to be left by himself. Usually he could be coaxed into it, even if it took a while. It was harder at night, when he didn't want to be put to sleep.

One way or another, we couldn't go without Grandfather's teeth.

We tried talking to him. Nothing worked. I told Pan Jozek that we had to do something to startle Grandfather so much that he would open his mouth like a shocked child. Then we could grab his teeth. We didn't have to worry about being bitten, I explained, because Grandfather took a long time to react. He took a long time to do anything, whether it was walking, talking, or thinking. You could say three whole Paternosters between the time he had a thought and the time he put it into words.

"What do you do to startle him?" asked Pan Jozek.

"We suddenly jump on him," I said. "Or I stand on my head and kick my feet. It depends on who's here. Antony just picks him up and lifts him in the air."

I debated whether to tell him about Grandmother. I couldn't resist. "And my grandmother," I said, "does something really vulgar."

As soon as he asked me to tell him what that was I felt sorry I had said it, because what Grandmother did was to lift all her skirts at once and turn around to show Grandfather her bare bottom while I snatched the teeth from his mouth. It was easy as pie.

Pan Jozek took a look around the room and said, "Marek, I've got it!"

He took Grandfather's umbrella, which was standing in a corner by the door, told me to be ready, and went over to Grandfather. I had no idea what he was about to do. Suddenly he opened the umbrella right in Grandfather's face. Grandfather was so flabbergasted that his mouth dropped open long enough for me to grab his teeth.

That kind of trick worked well enough as long as Grandfather stayed in his fog. Sometimes, though, he snapped out of it and became his old self again. If we tried fooling him then, or treating him like a child by spoon-feeding or undressing him for bed, he would give us a shrewd look as if to ask how we could be so shameless. At times like that I felt like crawling into the ground.

Sometimes he would become lucid again for only a few minutes, other times for hours at a time. It might even last a few days, as if there were nothing wrong with him. When that happened he was shocked by how much time he had lost, because he couldn't remember a thing since he had last lost track of himself. Everything in between was wiped out, whether it was a few days, a week, or several weeks. He would sit up and wonder what had happened to all that time and ask how the war was getting on.

I remember one time when Grandmother and I used Grandmother's method to get his teeth. All at once he snapped out of his trance, looked at us both, and said to her, "What do you think you're doing? Aren't you ashamed of yourself? Why, Marek is standing right here! And you, Marek, what are you trying to do to me? How dare you? Give me my teeth. Go home this minute and don't come back until I've had a talk with your mother!"

I brought Pan Jozek to Pan Korek's. Pan Korek took an instant liking to him. He promised to bring down an old crate of books from the attic so that he could have something to read.

I gave Pan Korek the money and went home.

8

Moving Pan Jozek

For two months everything went smoothly. Until the beginning of April you might have thought I had forgotten all about Pan Jozek, because I wasn't allowed to see him even when I was working in the tavern. Once or twice I took some of the remaining money from its hiding place and brought it to Pan Korek.

And then one day I found my mother waiting for me at the school gate after class. Although I could see right away that she was all right, I was frightened nonetheless. When we had walked away from all the children, she told me what was the matter. Pan Korek had had a bad quarrel, complete with curses and blows, with Pan Szczupak. Pan Szczupak was a known informer. He had worked for the police even before the war, and now he worked for the Germans too. He was high up on Antony's black list.

Although Pan Szczupak was a regular customer in the tavern and had never informed on anyone who drank there, perhaps because he was given all his drinks at half price, Pan Korek was frightened. He was, after all, hiding Jews — and not just Pan Jozek.

Of course, Pan Szczupak knew nothing about this, but if he were to pin some rap on Pan Korek and Pan Korek's apartment were searched, the Jews would be found. Even if Jews were a good source of income and Pan Korek turned his over to the underground, no one was ready to get killed because of them. And so Pan Korek phoned my mother at her sewing shop and asked her to come at once to pick up her "merchandise." My mother went first to my Uncle Wladislaw's, but there was still no room there. Even the emergency place that my uncle kept for a "temporary," someone who was willing to pay extra for a short stay, would not be available for another week to ten days. That was when my mother told me to go speak to my grandmother. She began to instruct me how to talk to her, but I told her that I didn't need any lessons.

My grandparents' apartment was of course an ideal place to hide Pan Jozek in. Even if someone saw him enter it with us, he would be taken for a doctor visiting Grandfather.

After thinking it over, we decided on a story to tell Grandmother. Since it wasn't easy to put one over on her, we decided to tell her the truth, or rather a slightly improved version of it. We would say that Pan Jozek was an ex-teacher of mine whom I had run into in the street, and that although we knew he was Jewish, we felt we had to help him. All he needed was somewhere to stay for a week to ten days until a place being prepared for him by some friends was ready, and he was quite willing to pay for it. We couldn't take him home with us because of Antony, who mustn't know about it, quite apart from the fact that our doorman, Valenty, might suspect something.

I took a streetcar to Theater Square. Grandmother was sitting in her usual chair. I gave her a kiss, though I knew it would warn her that I wanted something. I did want something, and anyway, she liked to be kissed even if it put her guard up. She shook her finger at me and said, "I'm all out of money, and all out of sardines, and all out of everything, Marek. What is it that you want from me, my darling?" That kind of talk meant she was in a good mood.

"Grandma," I said, "this time it's serious. But first I have to ask you something."

She looked at me without a word. So I started in on Jesus and Mary. I asked her if she knew that they were Jews just like the Jews in the ghetto.

She would have slapped my face then and there if she could have done it sitting down.

"Like the Jews in the ghetto? Our Lord Jesus and the Virgin Mary? What kind of blasphemy is that, Marek? How can you kiss me and then make me so upset? I have a headache from you already!"

She clutched her head with both hands but went on looking at me curiously. So I told her the "story," and she fell for it. I was very proud of myself.

"It's only for a few days, Grandma," I said. "We'll have to get him out of here by Saturday at the latest, because on Sunday we'll come as usual with Antony, and he mustn't suspect anything."

"Why did your mother send you instead of talking to me herself?"

"You weren't listening, Grandma! He was my teacher, not my mother's. She's just trying to be helpful."

"I understand all that. But a body would think she could at least have come with you."

"Don't you know that she's afraid of you?" I said.

Grandmother laughed. I could see she got a kick out of that. But what would happen, she wanted to know, if Antony found out?

"He won't," I answered. "He'd better not!"

She wanted to know what the Jew looked like.

"He's not the kind of Jew you're thinking of, Grandma. He's a different kind. He looks just like us. Before the war he was a medical student."

"Suppose I should have to hide someone from the underground while he's still with me?"

"But you can't even tell he's a Jew, Grandma. If anyone asks you can always say he's a relative who needs to lay low in Warsaw for a week before moving on. You'll think of something. Or else he will."

"If Antony finds out, he'll throw you all out of the house!"

"He certainly will," I agreed. "And you wouldn't want him to do that, would you?"

"No," said Grandmother, half to herself, "I wouldn't want him to do that."

She sat there thinking. I had no patience to wait for her answer, and to make matters worse, a customer arrived just then and began bargaining for some

German cigarettes. He was followed by someone else, to whom Grandmother sold some matches and whispered something in his ear. Before anyone else could come along I asked, "Is it all right then, Grandma?"

"Tell your mother I want to talk to her."

I didn't like the thought of that. If my mother arrived there would be a big quarrel and nothing would come of it. Grandmother saw that I looked worried and told me not to be.

"Everything will be fine, Marek. I just want her to come and ask me herself. And don't go telling me it's not her business."

The fact was that I was equally afraid my mother would refuse to come. I knew perfectly well what happened when the two of them got together. All hell broke loose. If they didn't have something handy to fight over, they would manage to invent it. Before we were very far into a visit to my grandparents' my mother would lose her temper and become a different person. It never happened with anyone else. If the visit was short, it would end with them both in a huff. If it was long enough, there would be time to kiss and make up until the next visit. It didn't matter how often my mother swore beforehand that "this time" she wouldn't fight with Grandmother but would be nice and avoid any topic that might lead to an argument and insults. In fact, Antony and I thought it best for her to start arguing as soon as she walked in, since that left more time for a reconciliation. If she and Grandmother argued at the end of a visit, we might have to cancel next Sunday's dinner entirely.

Grandmother thought that my mother was a flaming radical, and my mother thought that Grandmother was a right-wing nationalist and practically a fascist. The truth of the matter was, I think, that they were still fighting over my father, over my mother's living in sin with him, and over my grandmother's cutting all ties with her — which was something, my mother insisted, that no real mother would ever do.

They fought over religion too. My grandmother considered my mother "a bad Catholic" even though she went to church on Sundays, and my mother believed that my grandmother was "a superstitious old fanatic." She also accused her of not taking good care of my grandfather, whom she left alone by himself all day long while she sat in the marketplace. My mother and even Uncle Wladislaw had offered to give Grandmother enough money each month for her to stop selling cigarettes and stay home with Grandfather. Grandmother's answer was that she was not going "to live on charity," but we all knew that she preferred to be out in the world and in the thick of things, especially since that meant a role in the underground. Sitting at home all day long with my sick grandfather would have been worse than death for her. She wouldn't even agree to my mother's suggestion that someone else be paid to stay with him. As with the electricity and gas, as I said before I think this was less a matter of pinching pennies than of her being in the underground, because she often hid people in her house. Not Jews, of course, although once she did hide an English pilot. And my mother underestimated my grandmother's earnings, which were considerable, both because she had a good head for business and because she cheated her customers. She once stopped talking to Antony for a month because he said that she "did business like a Jew." We missed a whole row of Sunday dinners until he apologized. Besides, my grandmother said, if someone had to stay with Grandfather, why didn't my mother do it herself? It would be no great loss if she quit her sewing shop with its miserable salary that that lousy Volksdeutsch paid her.

My mother agreed to talk to Grandmother. "She always has to be the boss!" Mother said.

In no time, of course, they began to quarrel. What about? About my mother's clothes! How could a "lady" like my mother walk around dressed like a rag woman? She might be married to a Skorupa, but she must never forget she was a Rejmont! "And you?" shot back my mother. "Look at yourself!" I could see her open her mouth to say something else and think better of it. I was sure it was going to be about the way Grandmother and I made Grandfather give us his teeth. It was a good thing my mother caught herself, because Grandmother would never have forgiven my telling her how we did it.

Grandmother replied that if she dressed like a peasant it was because of her work and as a disguise for the underground. The truth was that she had simply gone back to dressing the way she had dressed as a girl in the village. Grandfather's illness at least had the advantage of freeing her from the role of Pani

Rejmont, the wife of the eminent printer, who went about, as she put it, "tied in knots" with garters and girdles.

In the end, they kissed and made up. That day my mother and I went to bring Pan Jozek to my grandparents'.

Although it was raining, we went on foot because Pan Jozek wanted us to. My mother held his arm, he held the umbrella, and I tagged along behind them holding my school bag over my head. She looked young enough to pass for his wife, while I could have been his younger brother hurrying after him in the street.

He was at my grandparents' for exactly ten days. They were special days for both Grandmother and Grandfather. Grandfather changed visibly for the better. Not that he grew well again. And yet he not only didn't get worse, which we were used to his doing so slowly but surely that hardly a week went by without our noticing, he actually became better. Maybe it was because Pan Jozek spent so much time taking care of him. As an ex-medical student, he didn't mind that kind of thing. He was used to it too, because after the Germans took Warsaw and expelled all the Jewish students from the universities, he lived at home with his mother for a while.

Suddenly Grandfather was bathed and shaved each day. He even seemed to have put on weight. I don't think he could have gained much in a week, but being cleaner and less neglected made him look healthier. So perhaps did his not being so lonely anymore. Pan

Jozek fed him regular meals and Grandfather obediently returned his teeth after each of them. And whenever his mind cleared, he and Pan Jozek played chess.

It was the weirdest chess game you ever saw. They played it all week long, picking up where they had left off at the end of Grandfather's last good spell. It wasn't the game itself that was weird, because it was played according to the rules, but the fact that Grandfather couldn't remember the intervals between sessions, which were anywhere from a few hours to half a day long, so that he thought that all the moves were being made in one sitting.

I think it must be very odd to lose long episodes of time. My grandfather could lose a day or more at a time. I once asked a doctor friend of mine if the same thing happens in sleep. When you sleep you sometimes also wake up unable to tell if it is morning or evening, or how long you have been sleeping, or even where you are. Suddenly you don't recognize your own room: the door is in the wrong place, everything seems turned around, and nothing looks familiar. Was that Grandfather's normal perception?

We told Grandfather that Pan Jozek was an old teacher of mine who had to hide for a few days because of the war; that is, we told him in his first lucid period after Pan Jozek was brought to his house. Most of the time, however, he didn't ask any questions. He thought Pan Jozek was his cousin Witek, who had died long ago, and kept asking him how he was. Grandfather had loved Witek dearly.

When I said something to Pan Jozek about time "getting lost" in this manner, he remarked that the most extreme case was death itself. Then he looked at me and asked if I believed in reincarnation. I had no idea what that meant, though, and he never raised the subject again. Another time I was present when he had an argument with Grandmother about the Jews in Warsaw before the war.

I visited my grandparents two or three times while Pan Jozek was staying with them. Once I found him with a map, explaining to Grandfather why the Germans were losing the war. When Grandfather was "all there" he was so normal that it could break your heart.

Grandmother saw the change in him too. She wouldn't have admitted it, but she realized that my mother and Uncle Wladislaw had been right about her belonging at home. There was nothing stupid about her — it just hadn't gotten through to her until then. After Pan Jozek moved to Uncle Wladislaw's she began coming home regularly for lunch and spending the rest of the day with Grandfather.

Grandmother fell in love with Pan Jozek. He stayed up with her to all hours of the night trying to help her make cigarettes. It didn't take her long, though, to see that she was better off without his help, and so she rolled the cigarettes herself while he sat next to her telling stories.

Pan Jozek didn't just have left-wing views. He had two left hands also. He tried so hard to learn to roll cigarettes like the rest of us that I was sure he would pick it up in a day or two, but when I visited again that weekend, he had made no progress at all. If he didn't spill the tobacco, the cigarette paper tore or the cigarette came out comically limp. Or else the tobacco tube didn't close. Or the rod that pushed the tobacco into the paper jammed — something I wouldn't have believed possible if I hadn't seen him make it happen.

He was just as funny when he smoked. To begin with, he never managed to light a cigarette with one match: either the match went out or the cigarette went up in flames. And when it was finally lit he held it and flicked its ashes so strangely that Grandmother and I couldn't look at each other if we wanted to keep from laughing, which in the end we did anyway. Pan Jozek didn't seem to mind. He thought it funny that we laughed. By the end of his stay Grandmother was laughing dotingly right in front of him.

Uncle Wladislaw could take Pan Jozek only on the second Sunday of his stay at my grandparents'. That Saturday night I slept at their house to keep Antony from wondering why I was going there so early in the morning. When Antony went home from church, my mother would join us under the pretext of visiting her friend Wanda. It was all planned logically. That night around the supper table I listened to Grandmother and Pan Jozek talk about the Jews.

After we had finished eating I cleaned off the table and sat down to help Grandmother and Grandfather roll cigarettes. I was a real expert at it. Grandmother asked Pan Jozek to join us, and after he told us about his day with Grandfather she asked him about his medical studies.

"It wasn't easy for a Jew like me to get into the university," he said. "There was a ten percent quota on Jews, though in fact even less were accepted. Only the best Jewish students got in. And afterward of course the other students hated them for doing so well."

Pan Jozek told us how the right-wing students slashed the faces of Jewish students with razor blades tied to sticks. Grandmother didn't comment. Pan Jozek himself was never assaulted, because no one suspected him of being Jewish.

"Even I wouldn't have suspected you," said Grandmother, who prided herself on being a connoisseur. "A handsome young man like you!"

She waited until Pan Jozek finally managed to light his cigarette and added, "If the Jews would only have listened to us and gone to Palestine, none of this would have happened."

"The Jews have their own political movement that wants them to go to Palestine," said Pan Jozek. "It's called Zionism. I don't believe anything will come of it, though. The Jews will go on wandering the earth until no one cares anymore about things like nationality and religion. How could they possibly establish a normal country like Poland or Holland or France? Just imagine a Jewish army!" We all burst out laughing.

"But there were Jewish soldiers in the Polish army," I said, coming to the Jews' defense. "There was even one named Berek Joselewicz."

Pan Jozek was amazed that I knew the name. I had heard it in a story read to me by my mother not long after she told me the truth about my father. Perhaps she had been trying to sweeten the pill by showing me that Polish Jews had been not just doctors, lawyers, and businessmen, but fighters too.

Grandmother remained unconvinced. "I still say it's their punishment for crucifying Jesus."

"It wasn't the Jews who crucified Jesus," said Pan Jozek. "It was the Romans."

"Really?" I asked.

"Well," said Pan Jozek, "the Jewish establishment of those days considered him a rebel, something like a Communist today, and seems to have recommended to the Roman governor that he be put to death. Crucifixion was the standard method of execution back then, just like hanging is now."

Grandmother shrugged. "Then why does everyone persecute them?" she asked.

"That's the fate of minorities everywhere," answered Pan Jozek. "Whenever there are problems like unemployment, housing shortages, or even the plague, the minority is always made the scapegoat." He spoke as patiently as a teacher or a priest.

Something he had said before still bothered me and I asked, "What did you mean when you said that one day no one would care about religion or nationality, Pan Jozek?"

"That's just what the Communists say," chimed in Grandmother.

"Not exactly," said Pan Jozek.

"Don't they say 'Workers of the world, unite'?" challenged Grandmother.

"They do."

"Are you a Communist?" she asked.

"No."

"Do you believe in God?"

He thought it over and said that he did. I let out a sigh of relief. When you got right down to it, the Jewish God was the same as the Catholic God. But Pan Jozek couldn't let well enough alone.

"I don't believe in the God of the church or the synagogue. I believe in a God who's more abstract."

He looked to see if I understood. I didn't, but I didn't say so.

"A philosophical God," he said defensively. "A Being that we too are part of."

That was too much for me. I think it was for Grandmother too, even though she nodded. "Can such a God hear prayers?" she asked.

"I don't think so," he said upon reflecting. "But there's no knowing. I don't believe that God concerns Himself with all the little details. At least not the God I believe in. And yet, who knows? Who knows!"

The conversation shifted to Uncle Wladislaw, to whose apartment he was being moved in the morning. Grandmother said something about "the houses we got back from the Germans" after the Jews were deported from the Little Ghetto and Pan Jozek said, "You didn't get them back, Pani Rejmont, because most of those houses belonged to Jews in the first place."

"Yes," Grandmother said. "But where did the Jews get the money to buy them?"

She was thinking what all the anti-Semites thought when they said that the Jews "sucked the Poles' blood."

"If King Kazimierz hadn't brought the Jews to Poland back in the sixteenth century," said Pan Jozek, "it would never have developed its economy and its industry."

"He brought them because no self-respecting Christian would want to be a businessman," said Grandmother.

It was strange to hear her say that. What about herself? And Pan Jozek couldn't resist pointing that out.

"He brought them to be merchants because the Poles were total illiterates, Pani Rejmont. Things have changed since then. Marek tells me you're not a bad businesswoman yourself."

"Whatever you say, they're always ready to work for less and sell for less and take the bread from our mouths," said Grandmother.

"If the Jews hadn't developed the Polish economy, Pani Rejmont, there wouldn't be any bread here at all, as there isn't, I'm sure you know, in many countries without Jews."

Grandmother said she wanted to go to sleep. It was a good thing, I thought, that Pan Jozek was leaving in the morning. Maybe that's why he had permitted himself to talk like that and to call her "Pani Rejmont" so often. Still, it was thoughtless of him. Suppose he had to return for another few days and

Grandmother refused to have him because of this argument?

Pan Jozek slept on a mattress at the foot of Grandfather's bed while I slept with Grandmother in her big double bed, as I did whenever I stayed over. I lay there thinking about what Pan Jozek had said about prayers and feeling sorry for him. If that was what my father had thought too, I felt sorry for him also. If God couldn't hear your prayers, you were the loneliest person on earth.

I was sure I would never stop praying and believing in Him and that I would never stop going to church. The workers of the world could unite all they liked, I would always be a Pole and pledge allegiance to our flag and none other. Certainly not to the Communists' red one.

When I think of the flag I always think of Uncle Romek, because he was the flag bearer in the Polish cavalry charge against the German tanks. When I told Pan Jozek about him, he said it was a shame to sacrifice so much human life for national honor.

Despite my fears, Pan Jozek and Grandmother were lovey-dovey at the breakfast table the next morning. Pan Jozek paid Grandmother the compliment of saying that while she may have had no education, she knew more in her little finger than all the professors knew in their heads. She had wisdom, intuition, and a lot of horse sense, he told her, and he added, "And you're a beautiful woman too."

Grandmother was proud. They were a real mutual admiration society!

I had never thought of Grandmother as a beautiful woman. My mother was beautiful, but Grandmother was just an old grandmother. When I think about it today, though, I realize that she couldn't have been more than fifty-five at the time. She didn't have a birth certificate, but in those days women had their first child when they were twenty. Grandmother may have dressed like an old peasant, but what are fifty-five years in a woman? Today many women that age seem attractive to me, including my wife. Pan Jozek was much younger than Grandmother, perhaps by twenty-five years or more, but he might well have thought her beautiful, even if I was sure he was only trying to flatter her.

I thought that after getting to know Pan Jozek Grandmother would think differently about the Jews. She didn't. But she didn't scrub the house down with disinfectant when he left, either.

9

The Quarrel

The next day, Sunday morning, my mother arrived and the two of us left with Pan Jozek. Crowds of people were out walking by the Wisla. Although there was no need this time to bunch up under one umbrella, my mother took Pan Jozek's arm again and I took hers to make us look like a family out for a stroll on a spring morning. Everything would have gone well if we hadn't run into Antony.

Spring had broken out all over. I plucked a green leaf and put it in my pocket for safekeeping. Not that boys my age still played "Green," but I was always ready to be challenged by small children. I don't know whether Pan Jozek saw me pick the leaf or whether the spring weather reminded him of his own childhood, but suddenly he turned to my mother and said, "Green!"

They fought over who had won. The only green things my mother had in her possession were her pocketbook and Pan Jozek's coat sleeve. She began to laugh and argue that anything green counted, but Pan Jozek insisted that it had to be part of a plant. I didn't butt in, although I had always played by the same rules as my mother.

In the end she gave in.

"And now," said Pan Jozek, "you have to give me one of your shoes. You'll get it back from me after we've rested a while on a bench." My mother let him have it.

When we were children, whoever lost at "Green" had to pay a consequence, like singing a song, or hopping on one foot, or kissing one of the girls. Wacek and Janek used to make me steal candy from the grocery store next to our school. That wasn't easily done, because the owners watched the children like hawks and didn't let more than three of them into their store at a time.

We sat on a bench looking at the boats on the Wisla while Pan Jozek told us how the war would end. Then he told us how all wars would end.

"One day," he said, "the planet Earth will be attacked by enemies from space. Maybe from Mars. Then all human beings will realize that they're earthlings and this planet will become their common home."

"We were so sure that the First World War would be the last one too," said my mother. "Who would have thought that it would take Martians to unite us?"

"It won't, Pani Aniela," said Pan Jozek. That's what he called her instead of "Pani Skorupa." "Wars will stop before that. They have to. The history books of the future will describe a strange, incomprehensible age of human life full of senseless slaughter and suffering."

"God help us," sighed my mother.

All at once Pan Jozek began reciting a poem about springtime and peace. My mother had tears in her eyes. Maybe she was thinking of my father. Antony didn't know any poems by heart.

Today I think that a lot of Antony's hatred for Jews, Communists, and book learning came from being jealous of my father. My father was dead, of course, but Antony must have felt that he still lived on for my mother. He loved her a lot, and I only poured oil on the fire by refusing to let him adopt me.

We rose to go. My mother slipped her arm back under Pan Jozek's and I walked on the other side of her. That was when we met Antony. I never found out what he was doing there or why he hadn't gone straight home from church. As soon as he saw us he froze in his tracks. I saw the blood drain from his face, which had his murderous look, and his big fists clench. My mother was frightened but good. Pan Jozek didn't understand what was happening. I told him in a whisper. My mother left us, ran to Antony, and said something quickly in his ear. He gave Pan Jozek the once-over but didn't say a word. My mother tucked her arm in Antony's. She wouldn't let him shake it off, and we walked like that to Zelazna Street to bring Pan Jozek to my uncle's. Pan Jozek and I entered the courtyard under the eyes of the doorman and his wife, who were Uncle Wladislaw's partners in hiding Jews and in other things, such as changing money on the black market. We climbed the old wooden stairs to my uncle's apartment, and my Aunt Irena ushered Pan Jozek into the little room that was set aside for him and sent me straight home. I was afraid to go there, though. I went to Theater Square to look for Grandmother, but she wasn't there. That gave me such a fright that I rushed to her house on Bridge Street, only to discover that it was a false alarm. Grandmother had simply begun her new regimen of going home every afternoon. She made me tea and we sat and talked, about Antony, of course. I told her we had run into him. She didn't say anything. She just nodded a few times, as if she knew exactly what would come next.

"What happens now, Grandma?"

She didn't want to venture any guesses.

"What will happen to my mother?"

She didn't know. Or else she knew and didn't want to tell me.

I went home with a heavy feeling. For the first time since Antony came to live with us I was afraid that he would beat my mother. That must have been what Grandmother almost told me but didn't. I wasn't worried about myself. It was all my fault anyway. But if Antony laid a hand on my mother, I thought, I would kill him. I would take a knife and stick it into him at night. I even began to think of how to dispose of the corpse. I had all kinds of ideas, most of them utterly absurd. I just couldn't stand the thought of Antony beating up my mother. Even today I think that if he had done it, I really might have killed him.

Already on the stairs I could hear them shouting, although they had been home for two hours already.

"You women are all the same!" yelled Antony.

"You're eaten up by your own jealousy!" screamed my mother.

"Why can't you get it into your head," shouted Antony, "that there are other things in the world besides jealousy!"

"Like what?"

"Like trust, my dear lady, like trust!"

By then I had reached the door. I put my ear to it and heard my mother say quietly, "I know you like the back of my hand, and Marek had to atone for what he did."

She had told him!

They didn't see me come in. Antony grabbed hold of my mother and began shaking her hard. I didn't know if that was beating her or not or if it meant that I already had to kill him. I couldn't tell if he had hit her already, either. There was no sign of it on her face. The windows were closed to keep the neighbors from hearing. Not that it helped very much. Antony was white as a sheet and my mother was flushed and disheveled.

"Take your hands off her right now!" I shouted.

Only then did they notice me. "Stay out of this," said my mother. "It's none of your business."

Now she was taking his side against me! I had never seen her in such a state before. Antony let go of her, grabbed hold of me, and slapped me so hard that I saw stars. My mother began to scream. "Look who's talking about trust! You talk about trust and then you hit my son!"

"He's already a man," said Antony, "and I'll thank you to let me educate him." He turned to me. "You're not going to put this whole family in danger, do you understand me? If I ever see you having anything to do with Jews again, you're going to get it."

"You're not my father," I said.

He gave me a scathing look and said, "You're lucky your father isn't here now." And with that he stalked out of the room.

Holy Jesus, I thought, she's told him everything! I looked at my mother. He had had a reason for saying what he did. And in fact she confessed. "I told him that you knew about your father, Marek. I had to, because otherwise . . ."

Otherwise what? She never told me, although I kept asking her for years.

Those two things killed me: being hit by Antony and being betrayed by my mother.

"I'm leaving home," I said.

"Where are you going?"

"I'll move in with Grandpa and Grandma. And don't you come looking for me there until he apologizes."

I went to my room and packed a few things in my old school bag. My mother followed me, trying to talk me out of it. Antony, she sought to explain, had good reason to feel furious. We should have told him.

"He would never have agreed to help Pan Jozek," I said. "He would have said it was too risky."

My mother didn't answer. She knew I was right.

"Don't leave, Marek. Don't be impulsive. You know Antony won't apologize. Certainly not soon."

"It's not just because he hit me," I said.

"I know. But I had no choice."

Now that he knew, that both of us knew, I couldn't stand his presence any longer. I walked out and slammed the door behind me.

What I really wanted to do was to cry.

10

The Uprising

It started on a Monday, exactly a week before Easter. I remember the day well, less because it was the day after I moved in with my grandparents than because of what happened in the ghetto.

When Grandmother came to wake me, my first thought was that it was time to get up for school. Right away, though, she said to me that I didn't have to hurry and could even go back to bed once I had stepped outside and told her where the shots she heard were coming from. Grandmother was hard of hearing in one ear, which was why, as Pan Jozek had explained to her, it was hard for her to locate sounds, just as it's hard to judge distances with one eye.

I opened the door and stepped outside. The shots were coming from the ghetto. We hadn't heard shooting from there for a long time — at the most a few scattered reports now and then. This time, though, it sounded more serious. Reassured, Grandmother went back to bed, while I continued to stand there and listen. There were some bursts from a machine gun. I thought of Pan Jozek. He was lucky to be out of there.

Maybe he would be one of the few Jews to survive this war.

I got back into bed and thought of what Antony had said about my father. I wondered what would have happened to him if he had still been alive. Would anyone have discovered he was Jewish? Were there people who knew and might have informed on him?

I couldn't fall asleep and got out of bed again. In any case, I had to start out earlier for school from my grandparents' than from home. Meanwhile, the shots grew louder and more frequent. I heard explosive charges too. Or perhaps they were hand grenades. I didn't know that much about such things. Then there were ambulance sirens — not just one, but a whole lot of them. I couldn't imagine why the Germans were evacuating wounded Jews from the ghetto in ambulances. Could it be something else? Had the shots perhaps been fired by the Polish underground and only seemed to come from the ghetto? I started to get dressed so fast that I put the wrong shoe on the wrong foot.

"Where are you rushing off to, Marek?" asked Grandmother.

Before I could answer she had already guessed and made me swear to stay away from the ghetto. She would have insisted on walking me to school if I hadn't promised to take the streetcar. She even gave me money for it. I didn't mind fooling Grandmother. She was always fooling everyone herself.

I walked down Freta Street as far as Swientojerska Street, hugging the wall of the ghetto until a policeman shooed me into Kraszinski Park. Even though he knew me from Pan Korek's tavern, he wouldn't let me go any farther. It was too dangerous, he said. And maybe he was extra careful because he knew me. Anyway, Kraszinski Park wasn't a bad vantage point. There was a German machine gun there with some soldiers who were firing long rounds down Wolowa Street, right into the windows of houses. I could see soldiers stationed along the ghetto wall every twenty or thirty meters. I asked some people what had happened.

"They're finishing off the Jews," an old man said to me.

"It's about time," said a young one. He laughed.

Before my mother caught me with the Jew's money and before meeting Pan Jozek, I would have felt the same way.

"What do you think," asked someone, "will they give us back the Jews' houses?"

"Why shouldn't they?" said someone else. "Didn't they do it in the Little Ghetto?"

"What's all this talk about 'giving back'?" asked a woman who seemed very brave to me. "Those houses belong to the Jews." Everyone looked at her suspiciously and a man sniggered and said, "She must be a Jew herself."

We had no way of knowing that not one of the houses behind the ghetto wall would be left standing. Nothing would remain of them but piles of ruins.

It was unbelievable. It seemed to defy the laws of nature. And yet there was no denying that a real war was being fought there. Now and then truckloads of German reinforcements and ambulances of the German Red Cross, their sirens wailing, drove past in the direction of the ghetto. And to think that all this was the work of the Jews! Jesus, I thought, I'd better run and tell Pan Jozek about it.

No power on earth could have sent me directly to school that morning. I walked on. All up and down Leszno Street stood sentries with bayonets fixed in their rifles, facing the ghetto wall. Some Ukrainian auxiliaries were trying to come on to several Polish girls who were on their way to the grocery store to buy bread. The explosions, shots, and sirens carried even as far as there. A girl asked a policeman across the street if the ambulances were for wounded Jews.

"Fat chance!" he said. He beckoned to her and I followed her. In a whisper he told us, "They're evacuating German dead and wounded." He looked at us for a moment and said, "You think I'm kidding, don't you?"

I didn't. The girl did.

"You don't have to believe me, young lady, but this time the Jews are fighting back."

Before the day was over some people were already calling it "the Third Front."

"Green!"

Nothing could have been further from my mind. Had it been anyone else, I would have ignored him or socked him. But it was our neighbor's little son Wlodek, and so I pretended to search my pockets before telling him he had won. That made him happy, because whenever I lost I owed him a piece of candy. I promised not to forget and he ran away laughing.

I told everyone in school what I had seen. Other boys already knew too. The only things we talked about all morning were the Jews shooting at the Germans and the ambulances full of German casualties. I couldn't remember when I had last been so eager to go to work at Pan Korek's, because I was hoping to hear more news there. And indeed, in the tavern too that night the talk was all about the Jewish uprising. New customers kept drifting in with fresh reports, and the need to outdo one another at astounding us drove them to all kinds of wild stories.

Or maybe it was not so much the need to astound as to believe that it really was possible, that it really was happening, because if the Jews could rise up against the Germans, we Poles could go them one better. Someone claimed to have seen a tank enter the ghetto. Someone else said that it was accompanied by two armored vehicles. A third person spoke of three tanks. Others had seen artillery pieces on the move, an airplane circling overhead. It even flew over the tavern. Each time it made a pass I ran out to look at it until Pan Korek barked at me to clean the tables.

And yet even on the first day of the revolt voices were raised against the Jews too. Someone said they had stockpiled arms airlifted from Russia in order to set up a Bolshevik enclave that would attack the Poles.

"Why should they attack us?" asked a customer. "Their fight is with the Germans, just like ours."

"You must be a Bolshevik yourself!" replied the first man.

The tavern-goers didn't know whether to laugh, because no one knew who the man was. He could have been a Volksdeutsch, or an agent provocateur. He had never been in the tavern before, and so everyone sat quietly while he continued: "Did you hear what happened over on Nowojerska Street? They put a whole block of people to death because they found some kikes in some house. The same thing happened on Freta Street."

That wasn't so, and I said, "You're wrong. They just arrested them for three days and let most of them go."

"Most of them? Not even half of them! And you know why they were arrested? Because the Jews went and squealed on the Poles who hid them. We risk the lives of our wives and children to save those vermin, and that's the thanks we get. Mark my words. Oh, I know them, I do!"

No one said a thing. Pan Korek sent me off to the kitchen to keep me from opening my mouth again. After the stranger had left, perhaps to spread his poison elsewhere, more regulars dropped in and the conversation picked up again. There was more news. One man reported that the Jews had burned German tanks with Molotov cocktails, and not just the tanks, but the soldiers inside them too. Someone else confirmed the story. Through binoculars, he said, he had seen German soldiers on fire running and screaming through the streets.

"Don't ask me what they were screaming. 'Mama!' I suppose, or '*Mein Gott!*' "

Those words affected me strangely. It had never occurred to me that a German might scream for his mother or for God. I thought that if one screamed, it would be only to say Heil Hitler! or something like that.

Pan Korek must have read my thoughts, because he said, "It's horrible to think that they pray too. That's more than I can understand. Or accept. At least they do it in German."

He looked around to see who was listening. Pan Szczupak wasn't there.

Before I left the tavern, two more men arrived with the news that the Jews had run up two flags in Muranowski Square, the Polish flag and another, blue and white one of their own.

I felt goose pimples all over me. There was a long silence. Then Pan Korek declared, "Well, that's the first Polish flag in Warsaw in nearly four years. We'll see lots more of them one day when we run them up ourselves, but meanwhile, hats off to the Jews!"

His glance traveled over us. He said, "The Jews will all die, but they'll have died with honor. Here's to the Jews who raised the flag in Muranowski Square! It's on the house, boys."

I ran from one customer to the next, pouring out glasses of bimber. I didn't drink any myself, of course. Pan Korek had promised my mother that he wouldn't let me drink. But I did join in the toast.

I had promised my grandmother to come home well

before the curfew so that she needn't worry, but I wanted to stop off at my uncle's on the way to tell Pan Jozek about the uprising. I told Pan Korek that I had to be home early and he let me go, even though the tavern was more crowded than usual.

My uncle opened the door and brought me straight into the kitchen. That's where he always took me when he wanted to have a private talk. He told me that he had visited my parents and that he wanted to know what had happened between my mother and Antony. He wasn't in the habit of dropping in on us and he must have noticed my surprise, because he added, "Your Jew wants to go back to the ghetto to join the uprising and is willing to pay anything to get there. I thought that maybe Antony . . ." He left the sentence unfinished. He wasn't supposed to know about Antony's smuggling business. Was that my mother blabbing again?

"He wants to go back *now?*" I had never heard of a Jew voluntarily leaving his hiding place to return to the ghetto — and at a time like this! I couldn't believe it.

"You may not realize it, but young Jews have been going back there to fight. The doorman downstairs told me about another case. But I wanted to talk to you about your mother. She didn't go to work today. I found her at home crying and Antony wasn't there. Was he at the tavern tonight?"

"No," I said. "He wasn't."

I suddenly felt both worried and sorry for my mother. I had already forgiven her everything. I wasn't even sure I felt happy that Antony had left her. I decided to go home.

"They had a fight," I said. "It was over Pan Jozek, because Antony saw us with him on our way here." I thought for a minute and added, "They were walking arm in arm. You know, to look like a family."

My uncle laughed. "What made you move in with your grandmother?"

I told him that Antony had hit me.

"How come?" he asked.

"To make me mind my own business."

"I told that ninny to tell Antony. Your grandmother also thought it would end badly." He looked at me and said, "You certainly have gotten your mother into hot water!"

I said hello to Aunt Irena and went to look for Pan Jozek in his little room. He was pacing back and forth in his stockinged feet and smoking one cigarette after another. My aunt and uncle had already told him what was happening. He was delighted to see me and wanted to hear about everything I had seen and heard in the tavern. All day long he had been standing by the window, listening to the shots and the sirens. I told him everything, even the things I would rather have skipped over.

Pan Jozek began to talk nonstop. I didn't have time to listen, because I had to run to my grandparents', take my things, and go home. I was worried about my mother. He talked on and on about the rebels and Jewish honor, how they were saving it for posterity and all that.

"But no less important, and perhaps even more so, is their having saved Jewish honor for the Jews! The Jewish people," he declared fervently, "have begun to fight back against the Germans."

I was infected by his enthusiasm. "My uncle says you're thinking of going back to the ghetto."

"I'm not thinking of it. I'm going. Tonight."

His mind sounded made up. He had decided to join the uprising. I didn't know whether to feel pity or pride. I was sure he would never get out of there alive. In fact, he didn't stand much of a chance of getting in there alive either. All at once I realized that it was my duty to bring him there safely. That was the least I could do.

"When are you going?" I asked.

"Your uncle promised to talk to your stepfather. I told him I would pay anything. As much money as I have. And I should think that your stepfather would be glad to get rid of me after yesterday. Not to mention your uncle, who's already gotten a three-month advance for me. I've been waiting to hear from them all day. Your uncle says your stepfather wasn't home."

Oh, yes, by the way, my mother had given Uncle Wladislaw all the money I had taken from the Jew!

"They had a fight and Antony walked out on her," I said.

"Your parents fought because of me?"

My parents! I said yes. He shrugged and remarked, "Well, none of that matters anymore." For a moment he seemed lost in thought. "You won't find many women like your mother," he said at last, and then returned to the subject of the ghetto. "If your uncle can't think of something by tomorrow morning, I'll go myself. I'll walk along the wall like any Pole who's curious to know what's happening and I'll find some way of slipping through. The Germans have thought a lot more about keeping Jews in the ghetto than about keeping them out. I'm sure I can outwit them."

"You don't stand a chance, Pan Jozek," I said. That's when I told him about our smuggling route.

At first he was skeptical. He thought it was too risky for me. I told him that I was used to traveling in the sewers once or twice a week, and that if Antony had left home, he had probably gone to his sister's and wouldn't be back so soon. I just couldn't take him at night, because I would never find my way in the dark. Of course, it was dark down there in the daytime too, but Antony had taught me to navigate by the manholes overhead, through which a bit of sunshine filtered. "I'll bring you there in the morning and come right back. Even if Antony comes home in the meantime, he'll never know I was gone."

"You'll have to let me pay you in full."

"I wanted it to be my present," I said.

"No," said Pan Jozek. "I want to pay you for it."

He wouldn't yield. In the end I said I would hold the money in trust until he returned.

We agreed on that and shook hands. The plan was for me to leave home as usual in the morning as though I were going to school and to take extra food and water in my school bag. I would loiter on the street opposite my uncle's until I saw him leave the apartment with my aunt and then I would go up and get Pan Jozek.

"How do we get into the sewer?" he asked.

"I'll show you tomorrow," I promised.

I haven't mentioned this, but one of the first things that Antony asked me and my mother after finding out about Pan Jozek was whether Pan Jozek knew our address. He didn't. I might have told him if he had asked, but he never had. Antony breathed a sigh of relief. He would kill me if he found out that Pan Jozek had been in our house on his way to the ghetto!

The only problem was that there would be no one to close the trap door behind us. That was a risk I had to take, though. If my mother went down to the basement before I got back, I would be discovered, but by then Pan Jozek would be in the ghetto.

I took the streetcar to my grandparents' and caught the last car home before the curfew began. That is, it wasn't exactly the last car home, because it stopped quite far from our house. I ran all the way and got there right after the curfew had started. My mother wasn't worried, because she thought I was sleeping at Grandmother's. She had been crying all night over Antony.

Over the years I've often wondered how she could have loved two such different people: my father, who was perhaps a bit like Pan Jozek, and my stepfather. And yet it was Antony himself who had told me on the nights I brought him home drunk from the tavern that "a woman's heart knows no reasons."

My mother hugged me. She asked me if I was still angry. I said I wasn't. Whatever had happened was over and done with.

"But I did leave work early without eating and I'm hungry," I said.

She made me something to eat and sat down with me. While I ate, she apologized for what had happened. She had to tell Antony the whole truth, she said, because it was the only way for him to understand why she had agreed behind his back to let me take responsibility for Pan Jozek.

"But why has he left you?"

"Were you at your Uncle Wladislaw's?"

"Yes. I went there to tell Pan Jozek about the uprising. He already knew about it."

"Wladislaw was here. He was looking for Antony. Antony wouldn't allow me to tell him that he was called away on some business of the underground. I was crying because I was frightened, but I told Wladislaw it was because we had a fight. And we really did have one yesterday."

"I thought Antony had walked out on you."

"How could you ever think such a thing, Marek? You're just not used to seeing us fight. That's something you don't understand yet."

"What did Uncle Wladislaw say to you?"

"That Pan Jozek wants to join the uprising." She nodded and paused before adding: "God help him!"

"So Antony's off on some job for the underground?"

"Yes."

"Having to do with the Jewish uprising?"

"No," sighed my mother. "It has to do with something else."

It suddenly crossed my mind that perhaps my promise to Pan Jozek had been too hasty. If anything were to happen to me . . .

I was worried about what would happen to my mother.

I went on eating while she told me how everyone in the grocery store had spoken up for the Jews that morning and how Valenty the doorman had said that if they held out for a week, he would take back everything he had ever said about them.

I told my mother what I had heard in the street and in the tavern. She sighed each time I described someone's pleasure at the thought of all the Jews being killed. All at once she exclaimed with open anxiety: "Who knows how God will punish us for all this, for having sinned against the Jews! Who knows."

Before going to sleep I kissed her and hugged her, and she kissed me and hugged me back lovingly.

"Don't worry," I told her. "Antony can take care of himself. He'll come back safe and sound."

I didn't hate him so much anymore.

I fell asleep at once, but in the middle of the night I awoke and tiptoed to my mother's bedroom to see if Antony was back. She was sleeping by herself with one hand on Antony's pillow.

I awoke several more times that night. Each time I went to the window and looked out at the dark street, thinking of the morning.

11

Stranded

I was so tired in the morning that it was all my mother could do to rouse me. But as soon as I realized the time I was out of bed without further prodding of the kind that I needed on ordinary school days.

Antony still wasn't back and my mother looked as though she hadn't slept a wink. I decided against taking Antony's miner's lamp, because he might notice it was missing. Instead I took an old flashlight I had once been given for my birthday and put it in my school bag with a bottle of water and several sandwiches.

A new problem occurred to me: how would I know if my aunt and uncle had left their apartment already? I should have thought of that in advance. My mother reluctantly prepared to go to work and left a note for Antony asking him to call her at her shop if he arrived. We were like most people in having no telephone at home, but we could always call from old Pani Korplaska's stationery store.

We left the apartment together and said goodbye in

the street. I tried to make it sound like any other goodbye so that she wouldn't suspect anything.

Since I had no way of knowing if my aunt and uncle were still home, I waited in the street for a while and walked right in the front gate, saying hello to Pan Kiszke the doorman. In the middle of the courtyard was a garbage pit that stank terribly. I ran up the stairs and gave the doorbell the ring that Pan Jozek and I had agreed on, and he came to open the door. For some reason, I still remember that doorbell. It was old and worked like a bicycle bell, the only difference being that the handle revolved instead of clicking up and down.

My uncle and aunt were gone and Pan Jozek was ready to start out. There was an eerie silence in the apartment. I asked about the Jewish family that my uncle hid in the back room, where he and the doorman had built a double wall with a hidden entrance under a bed. I often saw them in the mornings when I came on some errand from my mother, sitting in the living room and playing cards behind drawn curtains. Pan Jozek told me that he hadn't met them yet, because astonishingly enough, they had paid my uncle extra to let them return to the ghetto for the Passover holiday, which came a week before Easter that year. I later found out that many Jews hiding with Poles had done the same in order to spend the holiday with their families. Pan Jozek thought this foolish and irresponsible. He was sure the Germans had found out about it and decided the time was ideal for liquidating the ghetto.

I told Pan Jozek that Pan Korek had said liquidating the ghetto was the Nazi occupation force's present to Hitler, whose birthday was that Thursday. Most likely the Germans had thought they could finish the job in a day and had not counted on Jewish resistance. Pan Jozek thought about it for a minute and said that both explanations could be right. In any case, when the Germans moved into the ghetto, there were more Jews present than there should have been. Perhaps other Jews had informed on them. I've already said that it wasn't only we Poles who had our collaborators and informers.

At first Pan Jozek had planned to say goodbye to his friend the priest, but now he chose not to run such a last-minute risk. Instead he gave me a note and asked me to give it to the priest when I got back.

We set out on foot. We had barely reached the corner of Zelazna and Grzybowska streets, where the Germans had erected one of the loudspeakers they used for broadcasting announcements and propaganda that we Poles referred to as "woof-woofs," when we saw a large crowd of people. They were listening to a German broadcast about the Russian murder of captured Polish officers in the Katyn Forest. A list of the murdered men was being read, and we stood and listened to it with everyone to keep from standing out. Every now and then the announcer would stop reading and declare: "These are the victims of the Jewish Bolsheviks! The Jewish Bolsheviks killed our officers in cold blood! The Jewish Bolsheviks will stop at nothing to kill, to plunder, to slaughter women and children." Then he would resume the list of names.

German propaganda was so full of lies that many people refused to believe that the Russians had a hand in the Katyn massacre at all. They thought the Germans had done it and were trying to palm it off on them. According to Pan Jozek, the graves had been discovered soon after the German invasion of Russia in 1941, when the Nazis overran the Russian-occupied zone of Poland. The Russians had murdered ten thousand Polish officers, whose names were later published every day in the newspapers as their bodies were dug up. Now, however, the Germans were rebroadcasting the entire list to divert attention from the ghetto, where they were mercilessly exterminating every last Jew. They wanted the Poles to have their minds on other things, which would keep them from sympathizing with the "Jewish Bolsheviks."

As we neared our building I told Pan Jozek to walk past it, double back after a few minutes, and enter the stairway to the left of the gate while I engaged the doorman and his wife in conversation.

I knocked on their door and asked if they had by any chance seen Antony, because I had forgotten a note my parents had given me for school and had been sent home. They were used to my raising hell in school, but they hadn't seen Antony. Well, I said, I didn't have the key, but perhaps I would go ask little Wlodek's mother, because sometimes we gave her the key to our apartment. Out of the corner of my eye I saw Pan Jozek start up the stairs, and I asked them if they had heard any news about the revolt in the ghetto. I let them talk on and on, and when they had finished telling me all the things I already knew I ducked into the stairway and descended to the basement instead of up to little Wlodek's apartment.

Pan Jozek was waiting for me there. I wasn't worried about what the doorman and his wife would think when I didn't reappear. If no one asked for me they would forget all about me, and in any case, I would be back no later than when I regularly came home from school.

By the time we entered the sewer it was after nine. At once Pan Jozek began to slip and slide. He had never been in a sewer before, and I walked as slowly as I could while he got used to it. All of a sudden I was in Antony's shoes. I remembered my excitement the first time he took me down with him. I had felt like a big hero, like the Frenchmen in the catacombs of Paris in Victor Hugo's *Les Misérables*. Pan Jozek understood what I meant by that comparison, whereas Antony would have had no idea. He would have said, "All we're doing is walking through some shithole. What does that have to do with a book written by some Frenchman who died long ago?"

Today I know that Antony was far less primitive than I took him to be. And yet that was how he wanted to be thought of, perhaps in order to be as different as possible from my father, with whom he didn't want to have to compete.

We reached the first rest stop and sat down on some boards. Except for Pan Jozek saying that the fumes made it hard to breathe, we didn't speak to each other. They really did make you feel you were choking, especially if it was your first time. We sat listening to the sounds from Leszno Street over our heads. We were still under the Polish part of Warsaw. Pan Jozek asked how much farther we had to go. I told him that by Antony's reckoning it was three more kilometers down Leszno Street before we entered the ghetto.

At the second or third rest stop I remarked that there was too much water in the sewer. Perhaps, said Pan Jozek, the Germans had decided to flood it to keep it from being used as an escape route.

We could tell the minute we reached the streets of the ghetto, because it suddenly grew quiet up above. We couldn't even hear shots. Pan Jozek glanced at his watch in the light from a manhole and declared that it was already ten-thirty. It would take another hour or hour and a half, I said, because we were progressing slowly. Antony and I could cover the whole distance in less than two hours with heavy packs on our backs, but of course we were used to it.

There was a strange sound overhead. It wasn't an automobile. We stood and listened to it come closer.

"Tanks!" Pan Jozek exclaimed.

I had already told him about the tanks and armored vehicles. Now he was hearing a tank move into the ghetto with his own ears, followed by another, and another. Then it was quiet again. We kept walking.

"They're not fooling around," Pan Jozek said with

an odd joy in his voice. "That means they're taking us seriously."

He was thrilled even though he knew as well as I did that the Jews could not possibly win. Their defeat was a foregone conclusion. Tanks would just make it happen faster.

We were still under Leszno Street when we heard the tramp of soldiers. They were singing as they marched, passing overhead with a single rhythmic tread. All at once there were two loud explosions. Pan Jozek was frightened for a moment, but then he began to laugh like a madman, because right away we heard the curses and the screams of the wounded. And shooting. The Germans had opened fire with machine guns and automatic rifles. Then it was quiet again and the marching resumed. This time, though, no one sang. Soon we heard the distant wails of ambulances.

After a while we stopped to rest again. Before sitting down on a board, Pan Jozek took my flashlight to read the number that Antony had written on it. It was seven.

"How many stops are there?" he asked.

"Fourteen," I said. "Antony says it's the same number as the Stations of the Cross."

Pan Jozek said something strange then. He asked me, "What do you think, Marek, if Jesus were alive in Warsaw now, would he join the revolt in the ghetto?"

I didn't know what to answer.

He went on, "Do you think he would return to the ghetto to be crucified again?"

We were sitting in darkness so as not to use up our

batteries. The sewage fumes stung our eyes. I still didn't know what to say. And so he asked me a third question, "Do you think Jesus would be able to forgive the Germans?"

This time I did answer, and I remember exactly what I said, because there was no forgiving the Germans for what they had done. I didn't think that even Jesus could do that. And now it was my turn to ask something that was often on people's lips in those days: "But where is God, and how can He permit all this to happen?"

"Marek," said Pan Jozek, "a lot of Jews wonder where God is too. But God doesn't operate the way men do. His punishments for their crimes aren't conceived in terms of human logic."

"Then the Germans won't be punished?" I asked.

"They will be," he said. "But not with the kind of punishments we're used to."

"What other kind is there?" I asked.

"Think of what it will be like for the next generation of Germans, the Nazis' children, to know that their parents were mass murderers. That could be part of the punishment."

It didn't sound like a punishment to me. Suppose their children never even found out? A punishment had to be something real, like laying all Germany waste, for example. Of course, that would mean killing still more grownups and children who weren't to blame for what was happening in Warsaw, but anything less than that, like the kind of punishment Pan Jozek had in mind, seemed ridiculous when compared with what the Germans had done to us and the Jews.

Pan Jozek was worrying me. He was losing his footing a lot and breathing heavily. I was debating whether to move on or to let him rest some more when suddenly there was a loud boom very close to us and we both went flying into the sewage. I managed to lift the flashlight clear of it just in the nick of time.

"Are you all right, Marek?"

I was. We both rose to our feet.

"That was down in this tunnel," said Pan Jozek. "Back where we came from."

"Yes," I said.

"We have to backtrack and see what happened."

I didn't say anything. The same thought had occurred to me too. If the blast had blocked the route we came by there was no way for me to get back.

Pan Jozek tried wiping some of the filth off himself while I shined the flashlight on him. He soon saw it was hopeless and said, "It doesn't matter. Let's go."

He hoped, he said, that the blast had been not directly behind us but in some more distant branch of the tunnel, because sounds carried farther underground. In fact, that seemed so likely that I was ready to assume as much and head on, but Pan Jozek insisted we double back. And it was a good thing we did, because the explosion had caved in a section we crossed and left it sealed off in darkness. Pan Jozek said that the charge must have been laid in advance and that we were lucky it didn't go off when we were closer.

"Who laid it?" I asked.

"Certainly not the Jews," he said. "Marek, how will you get back? I should never have agreed to your coming. You should just have drawn me a map. . . . What are we going to do now?"

"We'll think about that once we're out of here," I said. "There must be other ways out of the ghetto, and I'll bet they're cleaner than this one." Yet even though I tried to make him laugh, I could feel the fear creeping into my voice.

We headed on. My head whirled with thoughts, mostly about my mother, of course. I imagined the look on her face when I didn't come home and Antony found the open trap door in the basement. He would realize at once what had happened. In fact, that was my best hope. Any Poles like me found in the ghetto would be shot on sight, but if Antony noticed the open trap door he would go straight to my Uncle Wladislaw's, and once he saw that Pan Jozek was missing too he would figure out where we were. Don't worry, Ma, I thought, I'll make it back.

We reached the last rest stop about noon. We kept going without taking a break. We walked in silence, broken now and then by some comment about the low ceiling. We were under Nalewki Street and had hardly any clearance. It was from there that Antony and I had sometimes exited into the ghetto to loot the empty houses.

"Nalewki," I said. Pan Jozek sighed.

After crossing a low, narrow passage on all fours, we reached a part where the tunnel became higher again, though we still had to walk doubled over. I promised Pan Jozek that soon we could straighten up, and before long we did.

I don't think he could have held out another half hour. He was at the end of his strength when we arrived. It wasn't just the physical effort. It was perhaps most of all the bad air. As I climbed the iron ladder I heard him wheeze and pant behind me and say in a rasping voice, "Marek, there's something I have to tell you."

He sat down on a rung of the ladder and waited to catch his breath. Then he said, "I'm responsible to your mother for your getting back safely. I want you to do exactly what I tell you. You have to promise me now."

I promised him without thinking twice. All I wanted was to get back. The sooner, the better.

12

In the Ghetto

I handed Pan Jozek the flashlight and told him to beam it on the Jews' trap door. Then I took the metal rod that hung from the chain and rapped on the door as hard as I could. I tried beating out the same rhythm as Antony did, though I had no idea who was up there. There was no response. And so we took turns banging with all our might on the metal cover above us.

Perhaps, I said to Pan Jozek, the house had been deserted in the uprising, but I thought we could open the trap door ourselves, because I didn't remember it being covered with heavy sacks or objects the way Antony covered ours, just with a smelly pile of dirty rags. No sooner did we begin to push than we heard excited voices above us. There were sounds of running and of someone shouting, first in Polish and then in Yiddish: "Who's there?"

The door was opened. The pile of rags was as I remembered it.

Pan Jozek introduced himself and told them that I had guided him through the sewers and was stranded, because the Germans had blown up the tunnel. The Jews nodded now and then and whispered among themselves while throwing suspicious glances our way. They went to call someone and we sat down uninvited on the rags, which were cleaner than we were. At last one of the three brothers appeared and recognized me at once.

"Why, it's Marek, Pan Antony's son," he said, pointing at me.

"But they haven't brought anything," someone else said disappointedly.

It seemed that Antony had promised to bring them some "candy" that day. That filled me with hope, because even if the tunnel was sealed, he was sure to find some other route and take me back out with him.

"Candy," by the way, was our code word for bullets. "Food parcels" were guns, "eggs" were hand grenades, and "sausages" were pistols. As for rifles, they were called "Auntie's favorites."

The Jews whispered among themselves some more.

"Where is Antony, Marek?" asked the brother who knew me.

I told him the truth.

"Pan Prostak!" he called out. "Pan Prostak!"

"Pan Prostak?" murmured Pan Jozek to himself in a startled tone.

The man called Pan Prostak appeared. He didn't recognize Pan Jozek at first, perhaps because of the filth, but Pan Jozek recognized him and exclaimed: "Edek, I hoped it would be you!"

Now Pan Prostak recognized him too. He reached

out gladly to shake his hand but quickly backed away.

"Come," he said. "The first thing is to get you to a shower."

"Wait a minute," said the other Jews, taking him aside to consult. There was some more whispering and constant looks in my direction while Pan Prostak nodded in agreement. Perhaps they were thinking of some way I could help them obtain the bullets.

Pan Jozek introduced me to Pan Prostak. He did it as formally as if I were at a dinner party. By now, though, I knew better than to shake hands.

"This is Edek," said Pan Jozek to me. "He's an old school friend. I know him from the good old days. What do you say, Prostak?"

Pan Prostak led us and we followed him. Although it was the same basement Antony and I had been in many times, it didn't look the same. It looked more like the air-raid shelter we had sat in back in 1939 when the Germans had bombed Warsaw. The Jews called it "the bunker." They were planning to seal off the entrance from above so that no one would know it was there. Shelves and mattresses were everywhere. There was even a well they had dug and pipes for air. Some men and women were busy with last-minute construction, and as filthy as we were, Pan Jozek wanted Pan Prostak to show and explain everything to us. Pan Prostak said that there was no time, however, and that we had to be brought to a friend's house at once. When some workers came over to ask who we were and where we had come from, he asked them to step aside and let us out.

"Excuse me," he said, "but I have to bring these two gentlemen to a friend's house so that they can wash."

My eyes met those of a woman standing next to us. We both looked at my and Pan Jozek's filthy clothes and at our wild mats of hair and smiled at each other, because "gentlemen" was hardly the word to describe us just then.

On our way Pan Prostak explained to us that the bunker had been built by 20 families that numbered 80 souls and had been successfully kept a secret so far. Because of the Passover holiday, though, many Jews who had crossed over from the Polish side or come from elsewhere in the ghetto to be with their families were now trapped here, so that 120 people had to be crammed into the available space. They could manage all right for a day or two, but it would be a disaster if they had to spend weeks there.

"Weeks?" I said to Pan Jozek. "Why, they'll choke to death in two hours."

He looked at me but said nothing.

Of course, there were air pipes; I had seen them myself. But there was no way they could supply enough oxygen for more than a few dozen people. I tried to imagine the bunker packed past capacity. I wouldn't have been caught in it for all the money in the world. Pan Jozek must have guessed my thoughts, because he suddenly said, "What would you do, Marek, if you were here in the ghetto with a child or two of your own?"

What would I do? I could feel my hands ball into fists.

"I would fight," I said.

We crossed several courtyards and reached Swientojerska Street. All of a sudden we saw a strange sight. Someone was standing on a ladder propped up against the ghetto wall and talking to the Polish side. I couldn't see his audience, of course. Perhaps it was down below in the street, or perhaps in Kraszinski Park opposite the wall. The man was delivering a speech. He could easily have been shot by a German soldier, but apparently there were none around. He was saying that it was up to the Poles to come to the aid of the Jews. "Come join us!" he cried from the wall. "Let us fight together, shoulder to shoulder! The time has come to do battle! The time has come for all of us, Poles and Jews, to unite! The Day of Wrath has arrived! Let us rise up against the German conqueror who has ravaged our homeland!"

And it really was *our* homeland, I thought. They might have been Jews, but they were born and raised in Poland the same as Poles. And so were their parents and their parents' parents before them. The speaker warned his Polish listeners to watch out, because soon the shooting would begin again, and finished by crying out: "Long live Poland!"

There was applause from the other side of the wall while he climbed down the ladder. I was glad Pan

Jozek had heard it. I didn't want him to think that all Poles were like Janek and Wacek.

"You see!" I said to him.

But Pan Jozek just shrugged. He asked his friend Edek what he did in the Jewish underground, and Edek answered that he was just an ordinary soldier, if you could call the resistance fighters soldiers at all. He was also in charge of the bunker. Had the passage through the sewers been difficult? he asked. He too was worried about the blast down there. I didn't know it at the time, but apart from bullets, Antony had promised to bring some Jews back out of the ghetto in return for a large sum of money. If anything happened to him . . .

Pan Prostak said goodbye and went back to oversee the work in the bunker. He was sorry, he said, that he couldn't look after us himself, but he was leaving us in the hands of his friend Pan Rappaport, who would take us to an apartment where we could wash, change clothes, and have something to eat. And that's what we did. I was even offered a fresh pair of shoes, but Pan Jozek made me clean my dirty ones and put them back on, because if I had to walk through more tunnels or make a run for it, I wouldn't want someone else's shoes on my feet. He took two big wads of money from his wet clothes and handed them to me.

"As per our agreement," he said.

I took the money and sniffed it. It was slightly damp and it stank. Who was it who said that money has no smell?

Pan Rappaport and his friends invited us to sit down and eat with them. Pan Jozek saw how amazed I was by all the food and explained that it was because we were eating the leftovers of the Passover seder. If those were the leftovers, it must have been some meal! It was hard to believe that at a time when the Germans had begun killing off the last Jews in the ghetto, these people had gone to such trouble and expense to prepare a banquet.

The first thing I noticed — so Antony hadn't made it up after all! — was several men sitting around with hats on their heads. They were the oldest men there, but there were also several younger ones whose conversation I tried listening in on. Pan Rappaport took part in it too. I couldn't make it all out, but it had to do with the story of a man who had escaped from a place called Treblinka. It was a real horror story, because Treblinka sounded worse than hell. The man said it was where the Germans murdered all the Jews whom they deported in trains from Warsaw. Pan Jozek put down his fork. He couldn't eat anymore. I told him he had to eat if he wanted to have strength, and after a while he began again, though you could see his heart wasn't in it.

Pan Jozek wanted to know how the resistance fighters were organized. Pan Rappaport explained to him that our sector, which included the brush factory, was divided into five teams of fifteen or twenty young men and women. I shouldn't dismiss the women lightly, he said, noticing the look on my face. He wasn't annoyed. He simply explained to me that they were pioneers preparing for a hard life in Palestine and that they carried weapons like the men. Everyone had a pistol, but there was not enough ammunition to go around, and no more than a rifle or two per team. There were plenty of hand grenades, though, and homemade bombs and Molotov cocktails produced by the cottage industry of Pan Michael Klapfisz and Partners.

After we had finished eating, a young man showed Pan Jozek how to use a rifle and a pistol. The whole lesson took ten minutes. I had my doubts whether anyone could use a gun after that kind of cram course. Certainly not Pan Jozek. Mostly he was shown how to aim. If a Jewish fighter was killed or wounded, or if any weapons were captured from the Germans, there might be a gun for Pan Jozek too. Meanwhile, he could fight without one. I myself didn't seem to count.

Pan Prostak called us back to the table, which had been cleaned and covered with a fresh cloth. Pan Jozek spoke first, although it was obvious that Pan Prostak had something important to say to us. Pan Jozek tried to convince Pan Prostak that a way had to be found to get me out of the ghetto. Pan Prostak listened, but in the end he just shrugged and said, "We're all in God's hands now."

We both got the hint. When the fate of so many Jews was hanging in the balance, no one was going to go out of his way to save a Polish boy. Not many people, if any, were going to survive in any case. The person Pan Prostak really wanted to talk about, however, was Antony. He looked at me and said, "Your father hasn't come. Our people who do business with him say that isn't like him. What do you say, young man?"

"He's off on some job for the underground," I said. "If he gets back, he'll come. He'll come because of me."

"How will he know you're here?"

I explained to Pan Prostak that if Antony returned some time during the day, he would do his best to keep his promise, no matter how tired he was. That meant he would go down to the basement, and once down there, he would realize where I was. Pan Prostak asked how I could be so sure, and I said, "Pan Prostak, only Antony and I know about that trap door, and I left it open so that I could return. No one but he would notice that it's open, but he couldn't possibly miss it."

I didn't want to say anything more and he didn't ask me. If Antony found the trap door open, I explained, he wouldn't start out for the ghetto right away. First he would look for me in school, then at Pan Korek's, and then at my grandmother's and my uncle's. All that would take a long time. Besides which, he couldn't take the direct route through the sewers because of the explosion. But he was sure to find some other route and in the end he would arrive.

"It's not just the ammunition that worries us," said Pan Prostak. "It's his other promise too. He gave us his word and was even given an advance in British gold coins. I was assured he could be trusted."

Now that I was here, Pan Prostak said, I might as well know: a group of Jews that had crossed into the ghetto for the holiday had paid Antony an advance to make sure he would take them back. He had promised them that a truck from a building-supplies warehouse would be waiting for them by a manhole on Grzybowska Street at exactly 7:30 P.M., that is, half an hour before the start of the curfew. He also had arranged with some villagers to bring the Jews to a cabin in the woods where they could stay for up to a week, so that they wouldn't all return to Warsaw at once; they would have to make their way back there by themselves, which they could do because they already had forged papers and places to live. Some even had steady jobs. Such Jews were very wealthy, since it cost a fortune to arrange things of this sort. If German soldiers or Polish police did not happen to pass by the manhole as they were exiting, the operation had a good chance of going smoothly.

I knew that manhole well. We sometimes exited from it at night, back in the days when it was in the Little Ghetto. I knew the owner of the truck too, because he was a friend of Antony's who was given the warehouse at the same time that Pan Korek was allowed to move his tavern to an ex-Jewish storefront on Grzybowska Street.

As we were talking a young man approached and handed Pan Prostak a note. He read it quickly, glanced at me, and said, "Antony has gotten in touch via the usual channels. The deal is on, though he'll be a little late. There's a postscript, however." He read aloud from the note: "The deal will be called off if you don't take good care of my merchandise." That meant that Antony had guessed my whereabouts. I felt a wave of relief.

"Marek," said Pan Jozek, perking up, "you're going to make it out of here. Am I glad to hear that!"

"I don't know whether you'll make it out of here or not, young man," said Pan Prostak, "but we have to take good care of you until your father comes. We'll keep you in the bunker."

I almost jumped up and shouted no! I caught myself at the last minute, because I knew that my chances of getting away at the first opportunity were better if I behaved myself quietly. I simply couldn't imagine surviving with all those people and children beneath a ceiling that was barely two meters high. I was racking my brain to think of something when he added, "Which means, young man, that you're coming with me right now."

Pan Jozek shook my hand warmly. I wished him luck and promised him that if he got out of the ghetto alive, he would always have a place with us. Just let him come to my grandmother's and he would be taken in with no questions asked. Not that I believed I wouldn't see him again before Antony came for me, because there was no way they could keep me in that bunker.

Pan Prostak gripped my arm and steered me out of the apartment. "We're in a hurry," he said to me. "We've ordered everyone into the bunker by two o'clock, and I want to be there a few minutes before then."

He brought me back down to the bunker and

handed me over to one of the three brothers. It was the same man who had recognized me when I emerged from the sewer with Pan Jozek. Meanwhile, Pan Prostak checked the last-minute preparations. Before long we heard footsteps running down the stairs and loud, excited voices drawing nearer. A crowd of people burst through the narrow entrance all at once, sending us reeling backward. Before I could grasp what was happening, they were fighting for room on the shelves for their belongings. Wives screamed at their husbands, while the husbands shoved one another to the sound of wailing infants and frightened children. It was an awful sight. You would have thought that death itself was driving them from behind, although in fact each family was simply frantic that there wouldn't be enough room for them.

The quickest and strongest soon found themselves places and fortified themselves on their cots, while the others crowded together in the middle of the bunker by the tables and cooking areas. One of the three brothers shouted in Yiddish and waved his arms, but no one listened to his exhortations until finally Pan Prostak took out a pistol and waved it in the air. That made a great impression. Pan Prostak climbed on a table, and when the last family had pushed its way inside he asked for quiet and announced that everyone would be admitted whether they were paying shareholders in the bunker or not. But he was the boss. He alone could lock the bunker from outside, and he would do so only when all his instructions were carried out. The first of these was that nothing was allowed in except for food and blankets. The second was that the space would be divided up equally. (This set off a good deal of grumbling among the shareholders, but Pan Prostak took no notice of either the complaints or the cheers and declared that there would be no privileged classes as long as he was in charge.) The third was that everyone would get half a cot. "Half a cot per person!" he repeated. As for the food, it would be decided later whether to pool it or have everyone eat his own. It depended on how many days or weeks or months they would have to stay down there. When Pan Prostak finished speaking there was silence. It finally dawned on me how grim the situation was.

Just then Pan Jozek looked in to see how I was. We shook hands again amid all the shouting around us before he elbowed his way back out.

I looked around me. There were old men and women, families with babies, mothers with children of all ages, even people who looked educated and distinguished. For the first time I grasped concretely what the liquidation of the ghetto, which was something my mother, Antony, and I had often argued about, actually meant.

Pan Prostak was a shrewd, untiring man who knew how to get what he wanted. According to Pan Jozek he had been the manager of a large factory before the war. But as the bunker dwellers began collecting their excess belongings and carrying them back outside, he forgot all about me and I slipped out with the crowd and made my getaway.

Holy Jesus, if I had been shut up in that bunker any longer, beneath a ceiling I could reach up and touch, among all those people who were sure to start gasping in two hours, I would quite simply have gone out of my mind! I knew that no one would look for me. They had more important things to worry about just then. And once Pan Prostak had locked the bunker and departed, there wouldn't be anyone to look.

My mother was right, I thought. God help all those Jews, because who else could help them? God help them and have mercy on them, amen.

13

The Jews' Finest Hour

The Germans marched down the middle of the street as if they were in a parade. We counted them. There were nearly three hundred men. We were crouched behind a little window on Walowa Street, from where we could see clearly the main entrance to the brush factory. I was in an observation post with Pan Jozek and some other unarmed fighters. No one had told us what was going to happen.

It hadn't been hard to find out where Pan Jozek's team was positioned, because he was already known to everyone as "the sewer rat." As I climbed the stairs to him I saw different spotters at different windows and on different floors. Pan Jozek was shocked to see me and gave me a dressing down. When he was through talking, I said, "Pan Jozek, I couldn't stay down there. It was like crawling into my own grave. I felt that I was choking. Maybe if I had had little children like all those people did, I would have felt that I had no choice."

He looked at me and nodded sympathetically. "You'll stick with me now, Marek, and no monkey business. I just hope that Antony gets here soon. If I die, I want to do it with a clear conscience."

All in all, I think he was glad we were together again.

The Germans had reached a little square before the front gate of the factory. They were about to storm inside when suddenly there was a huge boom and everything went flying through the air. The fighters I was with were beside themselves. They laughed and shouted and hugged each other, crying for joy and unable to believe their own eyes. Everyone was trying to get to a window to see the scene for himself. The unbelievable was taking place.

It wasn't the first time that Jews had killed Germans. That had happened in Warsaw before, although not very often. Until the first day of the uprising such incidents were few and far between, however, whereas now a real war was being fought. The invincible, world-conquering German army was being driven back by the Jews! Of course, we all knew it couldn't last. No one had any illusions. But no one was thinking that far ahead. We had eyes only for the Germans crawling on the ground and hugging the walls of the buildings, hysterically firing in all directions while their dead and wounded lay scattered about, bleeding and screaming. I couldn't believe it. Pan Jozek put an arm around me and said, "If I have to die, Marek, seeing this will make it easier."

The Germans began to withdraw, dragging their wounded after them. They hugged the walls and beat a retreat, routed by an electronically detonated mine.

One of the spotters in our observation post had set it off. You could see how proud he was.

We received an order to pull out and crossed the street on the run under feeble German fire. Seeing me lag behind, Pan Jozek came back for me shouting angrily. I told him I had seen a German soldier knocked by the blast down some steps leading to a basement and that I wanted to take his rifle. Without a word Pan Jozek joined me. The rifle was still there. I was so excited that I almost forgot to take the bullet belt too.

I gripped the rifle while everyone regarded it jealously. Although Pan Jozek said nothing, the way he stared at it was so unbearable that in the end I let him have it. After all, I thought, he deserved it more than I did.

We were sent to a fourth-floor apartment under the command of a Pan Diamant, where I was given two hand grenades and a bomb as a token of appreciation. All three were homemade and had fuses that had to be lit with matches. The bomb was made out of a half-liter metal container filled with TNT.

I had a good throwing arm. I couldn't wait for the Nazis to come back.

I sat next to Pan Jozek while Pan Diamant put him through a rifle drill. He told Pan Jozek to fire only at clusters of Germans, never at single soldiers. That way he was sure not to miss. Two other fighters were stationed alongside us, so that if Pan Jozek was put out of action one of them could take his weapon.

Some girls came along with food and drinks to

hand out. I made myself take some, even though I wasn't hungry.

I'm not sure how much time passed before the Germans renewed their attack. It could have been an hour or even more. This time they didn't march down the middle of the street but rather hugged the walls in pairs. After managing to blow up the gate of the factory, they burst inside and a pitched battle began. The Jewish fighters fired on them from the windows and hurled bombs at them. For a while I stayed by Pan Jozek's side to see how he handled his rifle. He himself stuck close to Pan Diamant, who had been a soldier in the Polish army before the war and knew what to do. He took his time, too. The others kept urging him, "Come on, Diamant, shoot already, what are you waiting for," but he paid them no attention. He aimed carefully and every shot he fired was on target.

Pan Jozek was so excited that he shook all over. He got in his own way and kept using the wrong hand to cock and aim his rifle because he was a lefty. He had trouble with the sights too, which he complained made everything blurry, and after firing a single shot he handed the rifle to someone else. In its place he was given two genuine hand grenades and two homemade ones like mine, and we went down to the first floor to throw them from close range.

Those young Jewish men and women were not trained soldiers and did all kinds of things that no soldier would have done. Still, you could see they were ready to die and wanted only to take as many Germans as they could along with them. Some of the girls were only a few years older than me. One of them, I remember, was named Dvora. She stood on the terrace of a second-floor apartment and blasted away at the Germans without even hunkering down. She seemed protected by a magic charm, because no matter how much they shot back at her, they kept missing. Someone else bounced a Molotov cocktail off a German soldier's helmet, which shot up in flames and sent the man running on fire down the street like a maniac. He should have thrown himself down and rolled on the pavement, but his brains were too fried to work. I had just thrown the second of my two hand grenades when a German grenade flew through the window. A young man standing next to me picked it up and flung it back at once. His name was Luszek, and I never forgot it because he saved my life.

In the excitement Pan Jozek forgot all about keeping an eye on me. There was too much going on all around us and no one's life seemed that important anymore. I too got into the spirit of things and forgot all about Antony. I even forgot about myself. It didn't matter to me whether I lived or died. My own private fate no longer mattered and I was ready to be killed alongside the Jewish fighters. I don't think that was recklessness. I think it was self-transcendence.

The Germans began pulling back. Once more the Jews had to rub their eyes. To tell you the truth, so did I. The Germans were gone. We whooped with joy and hugged one another again.

What happened next was even more incredible. Three German officers stepped forward and asked to parley. They had white ribbons tied around their arms and kept their weapons pointed at the ground.

Afterward I found out that they had asked for fifteen minutes to collect their dead and wounded. They also announced that whoever surrendered would be sent to a work camp in Poniatow or Trawniki along with all his possessions. Suddenly several dozen people, most of them women, children, and old folks, stepped out into the street and gave themselves up. There were even a few young men among them. The poor devils! I don't know whether they had left that asphyxiating bunker or come from somewhere else. No one tried to stop them. We figured that none of us would live to tell about it anyway.

Even today I don't understand why the Jewish fighters didn't kill those German officers. It was hardly a time for gallantry. They should have let them speak and shot them dead. And in fact, a runner soon arrived ordering us to send five men on the double to a house on Franciszkanska Street, because the Germans had used the truce talks to break through our defenses via the roofs and attics there.

The Germans were shooting from all directions. So were we. But our firing was sporadic and we were running out of ammunition. So far we had taken few casualties, although only one of the men sent to Franciszkanska Street came back. Proudly he told us how the Germans had been fought from rooftop to rooftop and stairway to stairway until their advance was stopped. Once again they had retreated. But this time there was less joy than before. A lot of youngsters had been killed in the hand-to-hand combat, including Pan Michael Klapfisz, the news of whose death traveled from house to house. It was he who had set up a home-bomb factory. The young man who came back from Franciszkanska Street had seen him killed. He was cut down by a German machine gun firing from behind a chimney. So were many others before the gun was finally silenced.

Today, when I try to remember how much time all this took, I don't seem able to. The actual minutes spent shooting and throwing grenades couldn't have been that many, but each one passed so slowly that I can remember exactly what everyone around me was doing, whereas the long hours of waiting between one burst of action and the next have contracted to almost nothing in my memory.

I also remember the airplane that started circling overhead. Someone remarked that it was a bad sign, and in fact, it turned out to have been spotting for the German artillery that began to shell us toward evening. The Germans also sent small squads of sappers who started blowing up buildings. The fire spread to the adjacent houses, and we could see Polish firemen stationed beyond the ghetto wall to keep it from spreading still farther.

An order came to pull back to a bunker on Swientojerska Street. As there was a lull in the bombardment, our commander decided to withdraw via the rooftops. We climbed up some stairs and began to cross a roof. I myself was unarmed, while Pan Jozek had the pistol of someone who was killed but no bullets. He was hoping to find some. We were the last ones up on the roof and were starting across it on a chimney sweep's plank when a German soldier popped up in front of us. To this day I don't know how he got there.

"A German!" shouted Pan Jozek.

Someone with a rifle doubled back from the top floor of the next building, but he was too far away for a good shot. The German fired at Pan Jozek. Everything happened with lightning speed, although each time I picture it I see it lasting forever. Each one of the German's and Pan Jozek's movements drifts through my memory in slow motion. The German shot at Pan Jozek with a pistol. He must have been an officer or an artillery spotter, because he wasn't carrying a rifle. He kept firing again and again, standing on the chimney sweep's plank. And Pan Jozek ran straight toward him on the plank! It wasn't a long distance. He ran it with his arms held out in front of him, as though he had just seen a long-lost friend and were running to embrace him. The German grimaced. His face grew more and more contorted. He kept firing at Pan Jozek and Pan Jozek kept running toward him until he reached him. He threw his arms around the German, and the two of them lost their balance and began to tumble down the sloping tin roof. Each time they turned over and the German came up on top, he fought with all his might to free himself. He had lost his grip on his pistol, which slid down the roof by itself. He screamed. At the very last second Pan Jozek turned his head and our eyes met. I opened my mouth to shout something. I don't know what it was. Today I can't even imagine what it might have been. And then they were gone.

For a moment I stood there with my mouth open, listening to the German's scream grow more distant. Then there was a thud from the courtyard. The young man who had tried to come to the rescue reached me and pulled me back after him. I shook myself free. I didn't want to go with him. I had to get to Pan Jozek, at once. He was still trying to talk me out of it when a new bombardment began and we heard a shell shriek nearby. He let go of me and ran back toward the next roof while I ducked back into the building and ran down the stairs. Down below everything was in flames. The Germans had set the whole ground floor on fire. There was no way to get through. I ran into an apartment, looking for a blanket I could wet and wrap myself in. There was no water. I threw a blanket over my head, ran back to the stairs, slid down the banister through the flames the way children do at home for fun, tossed the burning blanket away, and ran out into the courtyard. It was empty except for Pan Jozek and the German. I ran to them. They were covered with blood. I tried to pull them apart, using every ounce of my strength. I can remember shouting: "Pan Jozek! Pan Jozek!"

His eyes opened wide for a moment as if with surprise, and I thought I saw the trace of an understanding smile. Then it was over.

I got to my feet and tried to pull the bodies apart again. It was impossible. Pan Jozek was still gripping the German as hard as he could, as if he hadn't let go even in death.

Suddenly there was a huge crash and a part of the house collapsed. I heard terrible cries from under the ground. They came from a bunker whose ceiling had caved in beneath the debris. Men and women began crawling out, dragging their children after them. The wounded had to drag themselves. I remember sitting there next to Pan Jozek and the German and thinking: What now? Where will everyone go? What will they do? I let go of the dead body and tried to help them, although I knew they didn't stand a chance.

I tried to pull a woman with a baby in her arms from the ruins, but the baby was already dead. For all I know it had choked beforehand. Then I lent a hand to an old woman. After that I remember only endless hands and faces, and voices, a jumble of them that I sometimes still hear in my dreams.

We pulled out everyone we could. The survivors told me to come with them. Someone said there was another bunker nearby. Someone said its occupants wouldn't let us in. Someone said he'd like to see them keep us out. His voice was full of menace.

"That's the rich folks' bunker," he said.

I asked a young man to help me separate Pan Jozek's and the German's bodies. The two of us couldn't do it either. Finally, a third man came along and we managed. No one even asked who the German was. Someone looked for his pistol, but his holster was empty. Once again the survivors invited me to come with them, but instead I started to drag Pan Jozek away from the burning building.

They trooped off. I could still hear muffled groans from within the caved-in bunker, but there was no way of reaching anyone through the debris.

The bombardment continued. And yet I felt that it had nothing to do with me. The sounds of the shells seemed to come from far away. I tried to wipe the blood from Pan Jozek's face. I shut his eyes and thought that I should bury him. I couldn't possibly leave him as he was.

He wasn't the first person I was close to whom I saw die. I had an old aunt who died when I was little. I remember how scared I was. And what I thought about then was the same thing I thought about now: was the soul still here, lingering by its master, or had it already gone to heaven? Long afterward I sometimes used to wake at night in a cold sweat and stare into the darkness of my room to see if anything was moving. I thought that perhaps my aunt's ghost was in the room with me.

I began to pray and stopped. What good were Catholic prayers for a Jew? But I couldn't not pray and I didn't know any Jewish prayers, so I began again. That was the least I could do for the man.

When I had prayed I hoisted Pan Jozek on my back and began to walk with him. I didn't stop to think what I was doing. I could feel his blood soaking slowly through my clothes and dripping down my shoulders and back.

I crossed a courtyard in which lay several half-burned bodies. The buildings around it were untouched and showed no signs of fire. Perhaps these people had caught fire in some hideout and been killed by the Germans when they ran out into the yard. I had seen things like that happen when Warsaw was in flames from the German air raids in 1939.

I have no idea how I managed to walk, or where I went. No memory at all. I just kept walking. Pan Jozek was getting heavier and heavier. Above me the sky was full of smoke, but down below at street level all was quiet. I don't even remember whether the bombardment continued or not. I don't know whether five minutes passed or only one. In the end I stepped out through some gate and ran into a frantic-looking man. At first he dodged me and ran through the gate. Then he came back and asked, "Aren't you Marek, Antony's son?"

I must have said that I was. Once he realized that Pan Jozek was dead, he tried to convince me to leave him behind.

"Where?"

He pointed to a corner behind us. I refused. "I'm taking him with me," I said. I wasn't going to abandon him.

"Antony won't keep his promise to get us out of here until he finds you," said the man. "Everyone who knows what you look like is out searching for you. There's no time to lose because the truck will come for us exactly half an hour before the curfew. Do you understand what I'm telling you? He won't take anyone until you're brought to him dead or alive. He wanted to look for you himself, but Pan Prostak wouldn't let him. He was afraid he wouldn't come back."

Suddenly it penetrated: Antony had come! There was hope after all. I might see my mother again. He had come to save me from this hell.

"Come on," said the man, losing his temper. "What are you standing there for? Let's go!"

He took me back to the three brothers' bunker. The door was open and its occupants had come out for a breath of fresh air. They looked awful, although to judge from how they stared at me, I must have looked even worse. I suppose that's because I was full of blood, even if it wasn't mine. Two men lowered Pan Jozek from my shoulders. They laid him on the ground and I sat down beside him. Pan Prostak and Antony appeared a minute later. I said to them, "We have to bury Pan Jozek."

"Marek," said Antony, "you don't know what you're saying. We have over twenty people to cross back with, and if we don't start out in ten minutes we won't make it in time. Do you hear me?"

I must not have responded, because he put his face close to mine and said, "It's me, Antony, your father."

"Pa," I said, "we have to bury Pan Jozek. I can't come with you if we don't."

That got through to him. He straightened up and said, "Pan Prostak, we have to bury Pan Jozek."

Pan Prostak thought for a minute. "Marek," he

said, "it's been decided to bury Michael Klapfisz tomorrow morning with full military honors. If we manage to do that, I promise you to bury our friend Pan Jozek along with him. You have my word of honor."

I believed him.

Michael Klapfisz was buried the next day, at 4 A.M., in the garden of the courtyard of 34 Swientojerska Street. A single shot was fired in salute. A year later he was awarded the Cross of Military Honor by General Sikorski on behalf of the Polish government-in-exile. There were fierce protests at the time by right-wing Poles in Poland and London over this "profanation of the highest Polish decoration." I was never able to discover if a second man was buried alongside Klapfisz.

Someone asked Pan Prostak if it was safe for the bunker occupants to return to their apartments for a while. He advised waiting another hour and then told all the people going with Antony to line up and get ready to move out.

I was given something to drink. I was offered food too, but I couldn't have gotten it down. I began taking off my blood-soaked clothes. As Pan Prostak handed me a fresh jacket I remembered something.

"Pan Prostak, there's a whole lot of money that Pan Jozek gave me in my pants' pockets."

"All right," he said. "I'll take care of it."

Antony reappeared with a package wrapped in wax paper. He took me aside and asked if I had managed to pull myself together. I told him I had. He asked whether anyone apart from Pan Jozek knew of the entrance to the sewer system in our house. At first I didn't understand. Then I said no.

"Why didn't you tell me, goddam it? I would have brought him myself. I had to come anyway."

"The hell you would have! And anyhow, I never meant to stay here. It's just that an explosion blocked the way back . . ."

I was shaking all over despite the dry jacket I was wearing. My teeth chattered. Antony went to bring me a blanket. He wrapped me in it and told me to lie down. I did as he said.

"You're still in shock," he said. "You'll come out of it."

"And besides," I continued, "you wouldn't have gone to get him from Uncle Wladislaw's. You would have said it was too risky to take him through the streets to our house."

"Marek, don't be a fool. The sewers can be entered in all kinds of other ways. Don't you realize you should never have taken him through our house?"

He pointed to the package wrapped in wax paper and told me to listen carefully. "There are some clean clothes in here for you to put on when we reach Grzybowska Street. Hold this package tightly all the way and make sure it's over your head when we wade through water."

I nodded.

Antony briefed me on what would happen when we got there. "As soon as we hear the truck pull up, I'll open the manhole and you'll jump out with me and two armed men. The others will follow and get on the truck. By then there'll be lots of curious onlookers. You, Marek, will pretend to be one of them who just happened to be walking down the street. You'll keep your distance from us. Above all, you have to look clean. You won't change your clothes until we're standing on the ladder beneath the manhole."

"What about you, Antony?"

"I'll do the same." He pointed to a second package lying against the wall. He looked at me for a moment and said, "You're still not yourself, son."

"How can you tell?"

"If you were, you'd want to know what kind of clothes I'm dressing you in."

He was right. I made an effort to smile, but my face wouldn't obey me. Soon everyone was ready. Our escort consisted of two young men with pistols and a young woman with a flashlight. She was the same person who had smiled at me earlier that day when Pan Prostak called Pan Jozek and me "gentlemen." Her job was to sketch the route we took so that the three of them could find their way back. Like Pan Jozek, they didn't want to leave the ghetto. They wanted to stay and fight.

We entered the bunker. Antony went over to one of the three brothers and was handed a baby. It was still business as usual! A cloth bag with the baby's documents was pinned to her blanket.

Antony hesitated for a moment before taking her.

"If the baby cries it will give us away," said a

woman member of the group. "This isn't what I paid my money for."

"Dr. Maier will give the baby a shot to make it sleep," said Pan Prostak to reassure her.

The scene that followed was familiar except that there was no tearful mother saying goodbye. The doctor bared the little behind and gave it a shot. The baby cried only for a minute. Someone said we should hurry up. As I helped Antony wrap the baby I detached the document bag and hid it in my clothing.

Someone opened the trap door and we began to descend one by one, Antony first and I next. Then came the young woman with the flashlight and one of the young men with a pistol. The other armed young man brought up the rear.

None of the group had ever been in a sewer before. There was one woman who began to scream and begged to be let out. Someone said that she was claustrophobic. It was only then that I realized I was too, but in a much milder form. The woman's husband tried to reason with her. Then he began to shout and to threaten that he would leave her and go by himself, followed by more pleas. Nothing helped. Everyone standing on the ladder had to back up and let the two of them climb out again. When the last man was in the tunnel I heard Pan Prostak shout something, first in Yiddish and then in Polish.

"Bon voyage!" was what it was.

Then I heard the metal trap door clank into place behind us.

14

Back Home

Antony was nervous and kept swearing at everybody, because he was afraid we would be late. It wasn't easy for them, though. To tell you the truth, it wasn't easy for me either, because I was exhausted. The worst part was where we had to wade through water up to our necks, although *water* wasn't really the word for it. Antony held the baby, his package tied to her bundle, over his head. His miner's lamp was strapped to an elastic band around his head instead of to his helmet, and his pistol and holster were tied to the clothes on his head too. It was the first time I had ever seen him take it with him.

We weren't alone in having a package of clothes. Everyone else had one too. They too would have to get back to their lodgings looking like normal human beings. Except, that is, for the two young men and for the young woman with the flashlight, who walked behind us sketching a map. When the water deepened she held her sketchbook and pencil above her head and several more pencils in her mouth. She too had her flashlight strapped to her head, where it looked

like a doctor's viewer. The three of them had no n
for fresh clothes because they were returning to t
ghetto.

As hard as our route was, however, the people with us made it only harder. One woman fainted and would have drowned had she not been caught from behind. Almost everyone had matches and a candle, but the candles kept going out, either from the air currents people made or from the fumes of the sewage. They also had trouble keeping both arms above their heads in deep water. Some threw away their candles and kept shifting their clothes from arm to arm. But no one swore and no one complained. Everyone knew it was a matter of life and death.

In spite of everything, we made it in time.

Antony and I reached the narrow ledge that supported the ladder more than ten minutes before our rendezvous. Antony sent a message back down the line for the second pistol bearer to come forward and told me to change my clothes. He was annoyed when I asked him to turn off his flashlight. In the end he turned his head away so that the light didn't shine on me.

"This is a fine time for your nonsense," he said.

"Suppose the truck doesn't come?"

"We'll cross that bridge when we come to it. Whatever happens, you go first."

My package had only four articles of clothing in it. That made sense considering how little time I had to put them on, quite apart from the difficulty of dressing in the darkness, in a narrow space I had to keep to was to avoid getting smeared with grime. I didn't have a second to spare. There were actually five articles of clothing, the fifth being a neckerchief to conceal my having nothing on under my jacket. It was stuffed into the jacket pocket and Antony had to point it out to me. In addition, there was a pair of pants, a pair of shoes, and a cap. Antony kept telling me to hurry up, because he couldn't change clothes himself while holding the baby. When I was done, I held her for him. He had the same four items as I did, except that instead of shoes he had boots. We threw our dirty clothes into the sewage and I thought of Pan Krol as I watched them float away.

Antony had also brought something else with him. From one of his boots he took out a jar of glue and a large mustache, which he pasted over his upper lip. Suddenly I no longer recognized him.

He kept looking nervously at his watch. The two of us might get away with it, but if the truck didn't come and left everyone stranded in the street, at least half the group was sure to get caught at once, if not by the Germans or the Polish police, then by blackmailers. And the others would never make it to their hiding places unless they found somewhere to change clothes, which they couldn't do in the tunnel because there was room for only Antony and me. I wondered whether Antony would suggest the back yard of the tavern, but at once I ruled that out. There would be too many people around.

Antony told me to take the baby. He showed me how to carry the bundle while I pretended to be an

innocent passer-by. I should hold the baby face do
he said, so as to leave her a breathing hole without h
being seen.

Just as Antony was slipping his pistol off his belt we heard the truck drive up. There was a general sigh of relief.

"Is this it?" someone asked.

Antony didn't answer. He simply crossed himself. So did I. Then he pushed open the cover of the manhole.

Everything seemed to happen all at once. It didn't take a minute for someone in the street to notice what was happening, and before long a crowd had formed all around me. I think that some of the people must have come from Pan Korek's tavern and were already on their way home. Fortunately, Pan Szczupak was not among them. I doubt that anyone saw Antony come out of the sewer, and certainly no one saw me, because I went first. That is, it later turned out that someone did see Antony, but the mustache made him look like someone unknown who had come to open the manhole for the Jews. The waning light of the cloudy spring day must have worked to our advantage as well.

The two young Jews stood covering us with their pistols while the girl stayed down below. "Jews! Kikes!" someone shouted all of a sudden. And yet I don't think that had anything to do with the two German soldiers who drove by just then on a motorcycle. It was just our bad luck. As the motorcycle stopped, the Jews opened fire. The last people out of the sewer ambled onto the truck, which was already in motion, assisted by the outstretched hands of those above. Two of them had lost their clothes packages. The onlookers dived for safety.

I ran with my bundle toward Pan Korek's tavern with Antony on my heels. Suddenly I sensed that he wasn't there anymore. I spun around, saw him running back, found something to hide behind, and watched what was happening.

One of the Jewish fighters was lying in the middle of the street. Antony ducked behind a billboard and drew his pistol. He and the other Jew fired away and wounded the two Germans, or perhaps they killed one of them, because he made no sound. The second moaned and cursed in German while the engine of his motorcycle kept running until the Jew stepped up and silenced him with another bullet. Then he and Antony ran to his wounded friend. They bent over him and turned him face up. Later Antony told me that he had been shot in the head. The Jew took the dead man's pistol and disappeared into the sewer. Antony shut the manhole after him and started running toward me. It was only then that I noticed he was limping badly. I tried to support him, but he said he could make it on his own. We both knew without saying that we were heading for Pan Korek's back yard. I gave Antony my arm to lean on again.

Pan Korek must have seen us through the window, because he was out the back door and waiting for us before we arrived. Antony told me to give him my bundle and explained to him where to bring it before

the baby woke and caused problems. He had been
he told Pan Korek, by a bullet in his leg. Pan Ko
took the baby from me and held her awkwardly, li
a man who has never held a baby before. "Does i
have a name, or any papers?" he asked.

"There was something pinned to it, but it must have fallen off on the way," said Antony. "Tell the mother superior that I'll bring her the money myself."

Just to be on the safe side, I had decided to give the baby's papers to my mother. I wanted the Jews to be able to find her after the war. But how would I know which child the papers belonged to? I thought fast and said to Pan Korek, "Her name is Julia Theresa."

Pan Korek smiled and said, "All right, Mr. Godfather, I'll pass that on to them."

I felt proud of myself.

I helped Antony onto the wooden seat of the three-wheeler. He told me to go fetch a blanket and some vodka. I ran inside through the storeroom and the kitchen.

Antony wrapped himself in the blanket, grunting from the pain in his leg. He took a slug from the bottle I brought and poured some of it over himself.

"What are you doing?" asked Pan Korek.

"Leave it to me," said Antony, pulling off his mustache. "I'll bet they'll have roadblocks up before we get home."

We set out. Although it wasn't a Sunday, as soon as I realized why Antony had doused himself with the vodka I knew that everything depended on our being stopped by local policemen who knew us.

ntony was right. Someone must have tipped off police, because right away we heard a siren in the stance and soon we ran into four policemen who arrived to cordon off the street. Without a moment's hesitation I pedaled right toward them and prayed. No sooner had they stopped us than one of them exclaimed, "Why, it's Marek!"

A second policeman, who was standing back, said with a chuckle, "I can smell Antony all the way back here. What's the matter, son, has your old man taken to getting potted on Tuesdays too?"

"Hello, officer," I said. "It's really no joke. I hope it's just this once. He'll catch it from my ma, my pa will!"

They laughed and let us through.

When my mother heard my usual Sunday-night whistle she was so confused at first that she didn't know what to do. I heard her frightened steps as she ran down the stairs, but as soon as I told her in a whisper to go along with the act, she fell right into the role. I don't think the neighbors suspected a thing. And as usual, their respect for my mother kept them from mentioning the scene afterward. As we dragged Antony up the stairs I prodded him to sing something, but that was more than he cared to do.

When the door was safely locked behind us, my mother threw her arms tearfully around me and began to ask how I could have done such a terrible thing. As soon as she saw that Antony was unable to get off the floor and lay there as if he were really drunk, however, she left me and ran to him. She

glanced at the pistol and worriedly ran her hand
him.

"It's nothing," he said, "just my leg. All that m
ters is that the boy is back."

She fell into his arms and Antony groaned with
pain. It was only then that we saw that both of his pants legs were soaked with blood.

My mother didn't stop berating me for a whole day, in the course of which I told her what had happened and explained that I had meant to bring Pan Jozek to the ghetto and come right back. Early the next morning I went to ask Grandmother to send us the doctor who worked for the underground. I had to tell the whole story all over again, from start to finish. She was very sad to hear about Pan Jozek and said she would light a candle for his soul even if he was a Jew.

After Antony had two bullets removed from one leg and some ricocheted slivers from the other, he felt much better. Within a few days he was ready to travel, because meanwhile we had decided to visit his sister in the country for Easter and perhaps even to stay with her for a while. It wasn't just a matter of being afraid that some informer might have seen us climbing out of the sewer. It was also on account of my mother, who couldn't stand the sight of the smoke hanging over the ghetto and the way it was talked about all over Warsaw.

I took a walk to the ghetto wall to try to see what was happening inside. There's nothing more horrible than seeing burning people jumping out of windows,

felt it was something I had to witness from the
sh side of the wall. I think the reason must have
en that part of me was still in there, with the Jews.
nd then too, I wanted to see what I had been saved
from.

All the houses in the ghetto were on fire. Their tenants were trapped inside them, and whoever tried to save himself was shot by the Germans and their helpers. There were Jews who jumped to certain deaths simply to get it over with. From where I stood with a crowd of Poles, firemen, and Germans, we saw a man step out on a balcony with two children. Everything around him was in flames. He blindfolded the children, threw them down one after the other — the balcony was on the fifth floor — and leaped after them.

Even before this, while I was still in the ghetto, the terrible doubt had entered my mind whether there really was a God. I remember how frightening it was, because I had to stay on good terms with God in order to get out of the ghetto alive. And yet the logic of it was elementary: there was no God. There just wasn't. All humanity, all life, was alone in this world, and whatever we did concerned only us and no one else.

When I think of it today, I know that isn't so, because pure logic cannot refute the feelings that I have. Not only when I pray, but when I search my soul as well, I find something there that did not originate with me. I don't mean to say that I feel God *in* myself. It isn't that. It's more being able to feel the vastness of Him *through* myself.

After I came home and my mother wept on my shoulder as if I had returned from the underworld (which in a manner of speaking I had), she kept asking me over and over to tell her what I had seen. In the end, she decided she had to go and see for herself.

The Germans allowed the Poles to stand outside the ghetto and look. They even permitted Polish children to stand next to their artillery and machine guns as they fired into the ghetto. My mother came back sick at heart, not only because of what she had seen, but because of what she had heard. Even those Poles who felt sorry for the Jewish children would often add: "Still, it's good we're finally rid of them." In Kraszinski Square, my mother told us, an Easter carousel had been erected directly opposite the ghetto wall, and Poles rode on it to loud music while the smoke of the ghetto swirled overhead.

At first the average Polish man in the street was so taken by surprise that the Jewish uprising filled him with enthusiasm. Even people like our doorman couldn't get over the Jews' courage. But the longer the fighting dragged on and the Jews who were left inside the walls kept it up, the more the citizens of Warsaw began to grumble about the smoke and the disruptions in streetcar service. They grew used to what was happening in the ghetto. The shots and explosions were no longer a cause for excitement. They were just something that kept you up at night.

My mother said that she couldn't go on living as if nothing at all were happening when men, women, and children were perishing in flames not far away.

Antony had reasons of his own for leaving Warsaw. He obtained medical papers testifying that he and my mother had pneumonia and that I had chicken pox and couldn't go to school, and the three of us departed from Warsaw.

One morning in the village Antony called me to his bed and asked me to sit down for a minute.

I sat.

"I have a question for you."

"All right, shoot," I said, because he had been unnaturally quiet for too long.

"Do you know what I'm going to ask you?"

I honestly had no idea.

"Will you let me adopt you?"

I pretended to think it over for a minute and agreed. I don't think it was because I had no choice.

"You can go on calling me Antony afterwards too," he said. "And bring me a glass of water."

I went to get it. I had had no intention of calling him "Papa" anyway.

It must have been the only time in my life that I saw him get emotional without being drunk.